His lips lingered close to hers

"Now," he murmured, "that wasn't nice of me at all, was it? Kissing my brother's widow before he's been gone barely a day." She broke the contact, jerking her head back to glare her hatred at him. He smiled, but it was full of cruel mockery. "Does that get rid of all those other softer descriptions you felt you should apply to me, too, like kind and compassionate, now that I've reminded you what a nasty rat I really am?"

She didn't answer him—couldn't. Her throat was too tightly locked by guilt and shame. He had mentioned Daniel, but she knew that if he hadn't, she would not have given her husband a thought. Not a single thought.

MICHELLE REID grew up on the southern edges of Manchester, the youngest in a family of five lively children. She now lives in the beautiful county of Cheshire with her busy executive husband and two grown-up daughters. She loves reading, the ballet and playing tennis when she gets the chance. She hates cooking, cleaning and despises ironing! Sleep she can do without—she claims she produces some of her best writing during the early hours of the morning.

Books by Michelle Reid

HARLEQUIN PRESENTS
1440–A QUESTION OF PRIDE
1478–NO WAY TO BEGIN
1533–THE DARK SIDE OF DESIRE
1597–COERCION TO LOVE

HARLEQUIN ROMANCE
2994–EYE OF HEAVEN

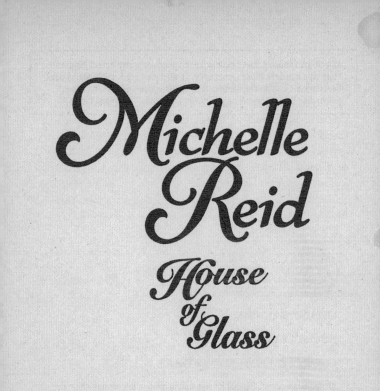

Michelle Reid

House of Glass

Harlequin Books

TORONTO • NEW YORK • LONDON
AMSTERDAM • PARIS • SYDNEY • HAMBURG
STOCKHOLM • ATHENS • TOKYO • MILAN
MADRID • WARSAW • BUDAPEST • AUCKLAND

ISBN 0-373-11615-2

HOUSE OF GLASS

CHAPTER ONE

SITTING with her hands twisted tightly together on her lap, Lily stared blank-eyed at her stark utilitarian surroundings. Grey painted walls. A pair of nondescript blue and grey curtains covering the window. Blue vinyl-covered chairs placed neatly around a small teak coffee-table scattered with old, well fingered magazines and a cup and saucer still full to the brim with a strong brew of tea she hadn't touched.

She'd been on her own here since the tea arrived. The young nurse had been called away to another emergency.

Emergency. She shuddered, closing her eyes against the memory of the urgent way they had worked on Daniel during that short, frightening journey here in an ambulance. The stomach-curdling wail of the siren as they raced through the streets. The shock, the confusion, the stunned bewilderment of what was going on around her. And, among it all, the young policewoman sitting beside her, gently urging out of her an account of what had happened.

The moment they'd brought Daniel in, they'd hustled her in here, the expression on the young nurse's face enough to make Lily's already horror-struck brain shut down in sheer self-defence, refusing to let her think, to even consider what the outcome might be. Since then she'd just sat here in the numbing silence. A silence aided and abetted by the dark grey painted door closed firmly against the busy hustle and bustle going on on the other side of it. Waiting.

How long didn't matter. Her own cuts and bruises didn't matter. The state of her clothes and the fact that she felt cold, icy cold didn't matter.

Daniel.

She gulped, seeing him as she had seen him last, lying twisted and bleeding on the ground. Fear shivered through her, settling sickeningly in her stomach and she gulped again, dry-mouthed and convulsively.

The door opened. Her blue gaze lifted to stare at it as the policewoman came in. 'All right?' she asked. Lily nodded. The policewoman glanced at the untouched tea. 'Would you like me to get you a fresh drink?' Lily shook her head.

The policewoman hovered, looking unsure what she should do next, then she walked forwards and touched Lily gently on her shoulder. 'They're doing their best for him, Mrs Norfolk,' she said, and turned and left the room.

Their best, Lily repeated to herself. But was their best good enough? She'd seen how Daniel looked. She might be in shock but she wasn't stupid. She knew.

God. A hand untwisted itself from the other and went up to cover her eyes. They were dry and stinging, her fingertips icy cold and trembling against her eyelids.

The door opened again. And the hand dropped away to watch the white-coated doctor walk into the room. One glance at his grim face and her heart stopped dead, her stomach revolting in fear once again.

'Mrs Norfolk?' he enquired into the thick silence in the room.

She nodded, swallowing drily yet again. Her anxious gaze did not leave his face as he quietly closed the door, paused as if bracing himself, then came over to squat down beside her.

'I'm sorry,' he began huskily. 'But I have some very bad news for you . . .' Reaching out, he gently covered her hands with his own. 'I'm afraid your husband died a few minutes ago.'

Even though she was expecting it, the news hit her like a blow to the chest, making her cower in the chair in outright rejection of it. Tears stung at her eyes then faded away almost instantly, shock falling like a veil of ice over her, forbidding her the ability to absorb the full horror of his words.

The doctor watched her, grim sympathy written in his eyes. 'If it's any consolation at all...' he went on inadequately, objecting—as his senses always would object, no matter how many times he had to do this—to having to convey this kind of news. And angry—angry at the useless waste of life. At the bitter sense of failure a desperate battle lost always filled him with. And overlaying it all was the gut-wrenching knowledge that not only had he failed his patient, but this woman, too—this pale young, blank-eyed woman who had placed so much trust in his ability to work a miracle. 'He never regained consciousness, so he would have felt no pain...'

'Oh, God,' she whispered. The face, the fine-boned slender body that did not look strong enough to take blows of any kind, never mind one of this magnitude, swayed dizzily, and she freed her hands to use them to cover her face.

Angry frustration clenched at the doctor's face, the bitter urge to hit out at something—the drunken monster who had mowed down her husband pref-erably—holding him tense and still while he waited for her to recover her composure. The swine had got away, of course, and, as far as they knew, with hardly a scratch. He had just climbed out from be-neath the twisted wreck of the stolen car he had been driving and taken to his heels, leaving this poor creature to watch her husband bleed to death.

'Is there someone we can get to be with you, Mrs Norfolk?' He uttered the next stock phrase they all churned out at times like this.

'What?' She still wasn't taking anything in. He could tell by the blank look she sent him.

'Someone we can call for you?' he repeated gently. 'A name. A telephone number?'

A name, Lily repeated foggily to herself, try-ing—trying hard to make her brain function. A name.

Mark, she remembered suddenly. Oh, God, poor Mark needed to be told! But he would not be an-swering his phone. He never did when he was working. He would be locked away now in his stu-dio with the telephone unplugged. Engrossed, blissfully unaware of the tragedy that had taken place while he worked. No, the only way to get to Mark when he was working was for her to go around to his home and——

'A close friend, Mrs Norfolk,' the doctor's voice intruded. And, despite not wanting them to, his eyes flicked down to his wristwatch, his mind al-ready drifting towards the countless other patients waiting for his urgent attention out there in the ca-sualty department of this big London hospital. Where was that damned nurse who was supposed to come in here and take over for him? It was ag-gravating, but he just had to get back to work. 'Or a member of the family, maybe...'

A member of the family—God in heaven. 'Dane,' she whispered thickly. And shuddered. She'd forgotten all about Dane.

'Mr Dane, Mrs Norfolk?' The doctor pounced on the single name eagerly. 'Do you have a telephone number or an address?'

Was·he even in London? Her fogged brain tried to recall the terse, brief résumé Dane had listed the last time they'd seen him. New York first, was it? Or Washington, Tokyo, Bonn? She couldn't remember. She hadn't been listening. She shivered, remembering just what she had been doing— drinking him up, tormenting herself, fighting that never-ending battle with herself not to let her feelings show: the fear, the hatred, and that all-consuming, utterly shaming need to——

Her hand jerked up to cover her mouth, sickness clawing at her stomach. Daniel was dead— dead! And she was sitting here thinking of——

'Mrs Norfolk?'

'Dane Norfolk,' she forced out from between stiff, cold lips. 'My h-husband's brother.'

She relayed the telephone number, which the doctor wrote down, but not before his bushy brows had risen in surprised recognition. So, she belonged to those Norfolks, he was thinking, and was impressed. 'I'll ring straight away; you just...'

'But he may not be there,' she added anxiously. 'He—he...'

The door opened and a nurse entered. On a silent sigh of relief, the doctor stood up to allow the nurse to take the seat beside the young woman and gently place an arm around her shoulders. 'It's all right,' he murmured reassuringly to Lily. 'We'll find him.'

Or someone will, he added silently to himself as he made his escape. Men like Dane Norfolk could always be found when it was necessary. It was just a matter of getting in touch with the right people. And there were a lot of right people—people in high places who would know Dane Norfolk.

Dane Norfolk let himself into his apartment and sighed heavily. He was tired, jet-lagged and fed-up. Tokyo had been frustratingly long-winded, New York a damned waste of time, and——

'What the hell——?'

A sound coming from somewhere inside what should have been his blissfully silent apartment pulled the two black bars of his brows together across the bridge of his long, thin nose. His mouth, already held in a tight grim line, looked forbidding suddenly as he stood quite still, listening, steel-grey eyes darting down his black and white tiled hallway from closed door to closed door until he detected the one from behind which the sudden noise had come.

It was then he saw it, the shiny black stiletto shoe carelessly left where it had been kicked off in the middle of the floor.

'Damn,' he muttered. 'Damn and blast it. The bloody irritating little——!'

Dragging a hand through his jet-black hair, he began striding down the hall, making for his own bedroom and knowing exactly what he would find waiting for him on the other side of the closed door.

The last thing he needed tonight was Judy playing seductress in his bed! He needed sleep—days of it—not the equivalent of a five-mile romp with an insatiable witch who had never understood the word 'enough'!

'How the hell did you get in here?' he ground out as he strode into the room.

She was lying—stark naked if he knew her as well as he thought he did—beneath a thin white sheet on his bed. The rest of the covers had been pushed negligently to the dark blue carpeted floor. Her hair—that long, silken pelt of vivid red hair—fanned out strategically across the pillows behind her so as to enhance the beauty of her exquisite face.

Exquisite, he repeated grimly to himself as he came to a halt at the bottom of the bed, pushed his clenched fists on to his lean hips, and ran his eyes over the seductive outline of her body beneath the cover.

'I asked you a question,' he snapped out coldly. 'How did you get in here?'

She pouted sulkily at his tone. 'Jo-Jo let me in,' she informed him. Then smiled appealingly. 'I wanted to surprise you. And I have done, haven't I?'

Oh, you've surprised me all right, he thought, feeling that all too familiar warmth begin to permeate his loins with a sense of angry frustration because he knew that, no matter how healthily his instincts were functioning, he was utterly incapable of doing them any physical justice tonight.

And anyway he was angry. Bloody furious, in fact, that she believed her position in his life so secure that she could simply swan into his home and his bed without invitation!

He gave no one that right. No one.

Without his expecting it, Lily's face swam up in front of his eyes, its sweet, placid beauty superimposing itself over Judy's lush features. And the warmth in his loins became a sudden consuming burn.

God, damn and blast it! he berated himself for that unwanted reaction he always experienced when he thought of Lily. He hated Lily's kind of beauty, despised the air of fragile innocence it so deceptively portrayed. It was all such a damned lie!

Yet he lusted after her with a hunger that privately disgusted him. And the fact that she—out of all the damned women in the world!—was the only one who would never be available to him only made the affliction worse.

Not that she knew it. Not that she would ever find out—not as long as his brother was alive would he let Lily know that he wanted her, sometimes with a desperation that drove him to drink himself back into sanity. And the fact that Daniel was seven years younger than himself made the prospect of him outliving him remote at best.

But he made sure she knew about his hatred. Oh, yes, he hated Lily. Despised her for the mercenary bitch she really was. He'd even told her that he knew exactly what she was up to—told Daniel the same thing in the hope that his poor brother would see sense and send her packing before it was too late. But Daniel was too besotted, too blinded by the masks Lily wore so serenely on her face.

Trying to save Daniel from a fate worse than death had only, in the end, managed to alienate him from his brother. He hated Lily for that, too. Just as that hatred increased when it had to be down to her that Daniel eventually forgave him.

Lily—Lily, the blight of the Norfolk name! he scorned.

'Mercenary bitch!' he'd accused her to her face— just after he'd purposely set about ripping to shreds those masks of innocence and purity she hid behind. He'd kissed her senseless, and, God help him, could still remember how bloody sweet she was to taste. He'd ruthlessly reduced her to a quivering mass of pure wanton in his arms before he'd stuck in his knife and twisted it. 'Daniel is the answer to all your problems, isn't he? He's prepared to marry you, he'll clear your father's debts for you without expecting much in return except the odd simpering smile from that lovely, lying mouth of yours and a quick on-and-off in bed!'

'God, you're disgusting!' she'd gasped. 'I love Daniel! Love him, don't you understand?'

But even now, two years later, he could still see the terrified expression in her baby-blue eyes, still feel the hectic palpitation of her heart beneath his grasping hand that told him more than anything else could have done that he was right about her motives for marrying his brother.

'Daniel is everything you're not, Dane. He isn't cruel and selfish and ruthless like you. He doesn't go through life hurting people the way you like to do.'

'He also has a very low sex-drive,' he'd put in scornfully. 'So, how are you going to cope when the bubbling furnace of those pent-up desires you so carefully hide from him boil over—as eventually they're bound to do? They would shock my quiet, placid brother rigid, and you know it. Show him even a tenth of what you've just shown me and he'll go screaming for cover in sheer horror of what his darling Lily really is!'

She'd spun her back on him then, guilt making her slender body tremble with self-disgust. And he hadn't been able to stop himself from stepping up behind her to pull her resistingly back against him, moulding her breasts in the palms of his hands, secretly revelling in their surprising fullness, their tight, firm shape. He'd dropped his mouth to her throat, inhaling the intoxicating fragrance that was uniquely hers, and sent his tongue on a salacious flick of her silken flesh at the same time as he pressed his body against her. She'd arched, gasping, unable to stop herself from responding.

'You don't love my brother,' he'd derided jeeringly. 'Or you wouldn't be responding to me like this. You love his money and what it can do for you and your thankless family!'

'Don't forget that Daniel gains a hell of a lot by marrying me!' she'd been forced to retaliate as she pulled angrily away.

'Oh, I haven't forgotten,' he'd replied. 'Daniel gets full control of the stud, as he's always wanted. But he would have got that in five years anyway. No. It's for your sake that you're marrying. Your greed, not Daniel's. God help him.'

'I hate you!' she'd choked, the wretchedness in her face wrenching at something obscure inside of him. 'You soil everything you come into contact with, and I hate you!'

'But hate or not,' he'd drawled, reaching out to touch a taunting finger to one of her breasts, where the nipple instantly burgeoned into pulsing life for him, 'you can't deny what I do to you. What will you do, my sensual Lily, when repressing all of this from Daniel gets too much for you? Will you have to resort to whoring to find relief?'

She'd slapped him then. And perhaps he'd deserved it.

'The way you do, you mean?' she'd spat right back, defiance shining brightly in her beautiful, lying eyes. 'Giving yourself to any woman who'll have you?' she'd scathed. 'You've no discretion, no bounds you would refuse to cross. You'll even go as far as to seduce your own brother's future wife! I may disgust you, Dane, but not half as much as you disgust me!'

'Disgust or not, you want me.' And before she could retaliate he had drawn her back into his arms and set about reminding her how easily he could reduce her to a trembling mess of mindless desire.

He would never forget the look on her wretched face when he had eventually flung her from him. 'As I said, darling, whore. Daniel's angel has whoring instincts.'

'And I suppose you're going to tell him what's happened tonight?'

No matter how she tried she had been unable to keep the frightened tremor from her voice. He'd enjoyed that, knowing she was afraid of him and what he could do to her clever plans.

'Would I be a good brother if I didn't?' he'd drawled.

And he had—told Daniel everything.

A smile touched his mouth, a wry, grim, sad excuse for a smile. For the first time in his life he had discovered what it was like to have his brother look at him with real dislike. Daniel hadn't believed him, of course—who would when you only had to look at Lily's sweet face to be blinded to the truth? Tiny, small-boned, short, straight white-blonde hair, big baby-blue eyes and Cupid's own innocent lips told their own story.

The wrong story.

'Bitch,' he muttered.

'That's not very nice, darling,' a petulant voice intruded.

Dane blinked, the angry mists clearing from his hard grey eyes, taking with it his brother's face and the echoing reminder of who had won the last round in his war with Lily Brennan, now Norfolk. 'I know Lily! And if she responded to you like that, then it's because you seduced her into it! God!' Daniel's disgust of him had cut deeper than anything else he could remember. 'Do you have to taint everything that's clean and beautiful, Dane? Just because Father went through life sullying everything he came into contact with doesn't mean you have to follow in his footsteps.'

'At least Father saw life as it actually was,' he'd sighed, 'not through the rose-tinted glasses you like to wear. For God's sake, Danny—see sense! Lily is using you—using you!'

'You think so do you?' Daniel had looked strange suddenly. 'Then that just shows how much you really know about her—or me, come to that.'

'I could have had her—right there on the bedroom floor!' he'd shouted furiously.

'Of course you could,' Daniel had flatly agreed. 'It is an inarguable fact, Dane, that you can seduce any woman you turn your prowess on. But what I never thought you low-down enough to do was try it on my fiancée—the woman I am going to marry! Have you no sense of honour or respect?'

'It isn't a case of honour or respect,' he'd argued wearily. 'It's a case of making you see her for what she really is before it's too late.'

'I know what Lily is,' Daniel had stated. 'She's the woman I am going to marry, and God help anyone who tries to hurt her, because they'll do it over my dead body, Dane. Over my dead body.' The warning was clear, the battle lost. 'So take your ingrained contempt for anything beautiful and leave us alone. I have no wish to see or speak to you again.'

And he wouldn't have, if Grandfather hadn't taken so ill. For the old man's sake they met in company, pretended there was nothing wrong between the two of them. But in private Daniel could barely speak a civil word to him. And if it hadn't been for their grandfather dying six months ago, the estrangement would still be there. Lily had coaxed Daniel out of it, convinced him that it was time to put old grievances aside. And, so help him, Dane was grateful to her for that if nothing else. He loved his brother. Daniel was perhaps the only person left in the world he could and did love.

He certainly did not love this woman lying so confidently in his bed!

'Get up, Judy,' he ordered. 'Get up, get dressed and get out of here.'

Without giving her a second glance, he walked out of the room and down the hall to his lounge, not stopping until he'd reached the drinks cabinet where he poured himself a stiff whisky.

'I don't know why I put up with you, you know.' Judy's voice had not lost its sensual drawl. Like the very sophisticated lover she was, she refused to take offence, even when it was thrust down her beautiful throat. 'You're so damned—moody!'

He glanced at her leaning in the open doorway, swathed in nothing more than the thin white sheet off his bed. Odd, really, he thought, but in the harsher light of this room she looked hard, the vibrant colour of her hair brash. And it occurred to him for the first time in several months' close association that the colour was probably achieved through a bottle. Her skin was good, though, he allowed, her body slender, well cared for. Tight.

'Why did Jo-Jo let you in?' It wasn't like his man to let anyone come in here without a damned good reason.

As a surprise for him was not a good enough reason. Jo-Jo knew that.

'Oh.' Her eyes widened on a sudden memory. 'He had to go somewhere pretty urgently—I've forgotten where for the moment, but he was in quite a state when I arrived. Something about a phone call and he had to catch you at the airport, but if he didn't, would I mind staying in case you turned up here? Of course,' that seductive smile overtook her features, 'I was quite happy to wait here for you. In fact, I could think of nothing I would rather do...'

Dane wasn't listening. He was frowning, puzzling over what could have sent his man tearing out to catch him in such a panic. 'Did he give you any indication at all why he needed to see me so urgently?'

'No.' Judy's creamy shoulders shrugged inside the draped sheet. 'Only to wait for you here and...' her eyes darkened with promises '... to hang on to you until he...'

The telephone began to ring. Dane stiffened as a sudden and strange sense of dark foreboding chased icily down his spine. He threw the remaining contents from his glass to the back of his throat then strode towards the lounge door.

As he went to pass by her, Judy put out a hand to stroke his jaw. 'Ignore it,' she coaxed, 'and come back to bed with me. I need you more than whoever is on the other end of the phone, Dane. Much, much more...'

At last some amusement sparked to life in his eyes. 'But Judy,' he chanted drily, 'you always need more—that's why you're such a damned good lay!'

'That isn't a very nice thing to say!' she cried, looking at him with big wounded eyes.

'Nice?' Dane repeated drily. 'Since when have I ever pretended to be nice? You don't want me because I'm nice. In fact, you would shock rigid any nice man, Judy,' he told her just before he brought his mouth down sensuously on to hers. She clung like a limpet—like a sex-starved limpet. 'Shock him rigid,' he repeated ruefully as he separated their mouths. 'Now, I told you to get out,' he clipped, coolly disengaging himself, and went into his study, pointedly closing the door behind him.

She would have to go, he decided. The woman was beginning to get on his nerves and she would have to——

'Dane Norfolk speaking,' he clipped into the receiver. 'Jo-Jo?' He straightened at the sound of the man's voice. 'What the hell do you think you're doing, giving that bloody woman free use of my home? She——'

He got no further. Jo-Jo interrupted him, his voice hoarse with strain. As Dane listened to what he had to say, that sense of foreboding became cold, hard fact, and he sank down on to the corner of his desk.

Nausea hit his stomach, followed by the inevitable sense-numbing shock. It began with a buzzing in his ears and travelled like marshmallow through his veins until it consumed all of him.

'When?' he asked thickly. 'Where? Was...?' He had to steel himself to ask it, but he did it. 'Was—was Lily with him?' He closed his eyes, fighting against an all-enveloping blackness which was threatening to assail him. 'Is she all right?' Followed quickly by relief, followed by the returning numbness. 'Where is she now? Alone? God!' he choked. 'You mean they've kept her there all of this time? What the hell are they——?'

Clenching his jaw shut, eyes tightly closed to offset the emotion going on behind them, he listened to Jo-Jo explain more fully. Then he heaved in a deep breath, pulled himself upright and nodded grimly.

'All right,' he murmured. 'I'm on my way... No.' He shook his dark head. 'I'm closer to the hospital than you are. You get back here and—and make a room ready for Mrs Norfolk... No, Jo-Jo,' he sighed. 'I have no intention of driving myself, but I am capable of calling a cab. And Mrs Norfolk will need me, no one else.'

No one else, he repeated heavily to himself as he strode quickly for the door.

Daniel—God—Daniel.

Just for a moment he had to stop walking while a vicious clutch of pain creased him in two. Then he was moving again, out of the study, and down the hall. Judy was forgotten. Everything was forgotten but the need to get to the hospital.

To Lily. Lily needed him . . .

CHAPTER TWO

AN HOUR. She'd been sitting here for over an hour
since they'd told her about Daniel, and still the full
crushing weight of it had not sunk in. A steady line
of changing nursing staff had taken their turn to
come and sit with her. They hadn't spoken much
and neither had she, and she was aware that they
were there to hold a watching brief on her shocked
condition as much as to offer a comforting hand
during this long, dark wait.

Lifting her head on a neck that seemed hardly
capable of holding its weight, she stared blankly at
the plain wall opposite her. A pain in her left
shoulder ran sharply down her arm, and she
winced.

The eyes of the young nurse sitting next to her
sharpened. 'You're in pain, Mrs Norfolk?'

Lily shook her head, lying because she didn't
want to be touched, messed around with, exam-
ined. Not in this place where Daniel——

Tears clogged her throat, inching wider the tenuous gap in her fiercely smothered emotions, placing a tight band across her chest as she fought to

contain it all. She had another ordeal to face before she could let go.

Dane.

He was on his way. A nurse had come in specially to inform her of it only a few minutes ago—or was it longer than that? She couldn't recall. Time seemed to have stopped meaning anything since Daniel——

Another swallow, and another wretched battle to maintain control. Daniel, who was nothing like Dane. Not in looks, not in character—not in any way that she had ever been able to recognise. They were even built differently. Daniel was slender and not so tall as Dane. His step was lighter, his moods sunnier, and he rarely ever let anything get him down. Dane was a big man—a looming kind of man with a hard-angled, shockingly attractive kind of face that warned of a great inner strength. Daniel had strength, but it was channelled in a completely different direction. His was a deeply personal and carefully hidden kind of strength that protected a part of him few even knew existed. But Dane's was all up front, and covered every facet of his life. He hid nothing, didn't see the necessity to because that strength said he didn't need to. And his step was firm, decisive, aggressive almost. Daniel was kind and gentle, with light brown hair and a fair complexion to go with it. His eyes were a bright sunny blue that twinkled with amusement a lot. Dane's eyes did not know how to twinkle. They were grey and cold, with those incredibly intimidating black bars for eyebrows that seemed to frown naturally. His dark, brooding good looks set women's nerves on edge because he reminded them so much of their adolescent fantasy man, the romantic, hard, ruthless hero they'd all at one point in their lives wanted to be totally suppressed by, yet were instinctively terrified of ever encountering.

Put them in the same room, and Daniel charmed while Dane awed. Just by the sheer height and presence of him he dominated the room while Daniel was quite happy to stand back and let him, that amused twinkle never far away from his eyes as he watched both men and women alike vie for his brother's attention, say stupid things because he made them nervous, flutter if he gave them one of his rare smiles or stammer if he frowned.

'With that kind of charisma, he should have gone into films,' Daniel had murmured to her once, watching his brother deal with the steady entourage of people who hovered around him. 'He'd be on his way to his hundredth billion by now if he had.'

'Heathcliff reborn,' she'd muttered, having to fight to keep the derisory note out of her voice.

'Or Rambo the Second,' Daniel had grinned. 'You've not seen his body. I'd kill to have a structure like Dane's.'

She'd blushed, and Daniel had laughed softly, chucking her teasingly beneath her chin because he'd seen the blush as a sign of her shy innocence.

He hadn't known then that she'd seen more of Daniel's body than she had of any man's.

She shivered, remembering the scene Dane had deliberately set up: a dinner party at his apartment—supposedly to celebrate his brother's coming nuptials; a guest bedroom set aside for her to use exclusively because she was travelling up to London directly from a visit to her mother's sickbed in a Devonshire private clinic, and she needed a place to shower and change; his arrival back early and the misleadingly casual way he'd strolled into her allotted room wearing nothing but a dark blue robe and carrying two glasses.

'Daniel will be a little late,' he said nonchalantly while she grappled with the belt on her own robe, blushing furiously because he'd caught her freshly showered, just leaving the bathroom with nothing but the brief robe to cover her nakedness. 'So I thought we'd share a glass of champagne before we get dressed. Here.' He held the glass out towards her, those cool grey eyes of his challenging her to come get it. He knew how she avoided coming within a yard of him if she could, how he frightened and intimated her, how he set her nerves on edge just to look at him.

She reached for the glass, and he held on to it for a moment, his long, strong fingers brushing against her slender ones. 'You don't like me very much, do you, Lily?' he murmured drily.

'I...' Like didn't come into the kind of emotions Dane sent rioting through her. 'I'm—wary of you, that's all,' she compromised huskily, then snatched the glass away, because she could no longer stand to have him touching her.

His laugh was soft and taunting. 'And do you know why you're—wary?' he mused, those cruel eyes of his mocking the oh, so revealing way she'd pulled away from him. 'It couldn't be, could it, Lily, because you know I can see right through your clever disguise?'

'Disguise?' she asked jerkily, not just wary of him but downright afraid. 'W-what disguise?'

'The one where you pretend to be the sweet, innocent angel for my brother while underneath you can't keep your hungry eyes off my body.'

'That's a lie!' she cried, but even as she denied it she felt the hot sting of guilty colour run into her cheeks.

Dane saw it too, and smiled cruelly. 'Is it?' he murmured, and reached out to touch a fingertip to the pulse beating wildly in her throat, and she jumped back in startled rejection, gasping because just that one fleeting touch had sent shock-waves of awareness rushing through her—an awareness she had been struggling with since she'd first laid eyes on him two long, wretched weeks ago, an awareness she had and always would put down to fear.

The laugh came again, taunting the hectic colour which rushed into her cheeks. 'I do find myself wondering, Lily,' he continued in that same lazily seductive tone, 'what you would do if I, say, undid that knot on your robe you struggled so hard to tie, exposed your beautiful body to my frankly curious gaze—then did the same thing to my own body? What would you do, innocent Lily,' he murmured challengingly, 'if I took you in my arms and moulded our naked bodies together? If I took those sweet trembling lips and moulded them the same way?'

'Stop it!' she gasped, backing off while he taunted, her eyes too big in her frightened face, his narrowed and glinting, challenging and cruel. 'Just stop it, Dane!'

'Stop what?' he drawled, those intimidating black brows arching mockingly. 'Stop trying to give you what you've been begging for for weeks? Don't be foolish, Lily. You know you want this—are sick with wanting it in fact——'

He went to reach out for her then, and it was sheer self-defence that sent the contents of her glass into his face. It surprised him. She could still recall the moment's stunned silence as he stood there with champagne dripping down his cheeks, over his compressed mouth, along his rock-solid chin. Anger flashed and she jerked another step back in absolute terror.

'Get out of here, Dane!' she ordered shakily.

'What, and waste all this lovely champagne?' Grabbing her arm, he pulled her against him. 'Lick it off,' he commanded huskily. 'It's your champagne, so lick it off.'

'No!'

Her protest was muffled by the sudden sweep of his mouth. And, God help her, she could still remember how sweet the champagne tasted on his lips, and inevitably on her tongue as he easily subdued her will to fight him.

She shuddered now, shamefully aware of how easy she'd made it for him.

She heard a soft thud as he rid himself of his glass by carelessly tossing it on to the thick creamy carpet. Her own glass followed, snatched out of her trembling fingers and discarded before he pulled her fully against him. And with an antipathy which throbbed inside both of them the kiss became a battle of wills which only helped to heighten the senses rather than quell them.

Then, 'Who is Mark?' he demanded against her lips.

'Mark?' She wasn't able to think, not of anything but him and what he was doing to her.

'You know,' he murmured sensuously against her questing mouth. 'The Mark you have a habit of meeting secretly several times a week at a small bistro not far from your house.'

She jumped, startled back to an awareness of what she was allowing to happen, and stared at him in horror. 'You've been having me followed!' she gasped.

His arms tightened, letting her feel the full potent force of his strength. Dane nodded grimly. 'I'm not Daniel, Lily. I take nothing on face value. And you, my dear, are just too good to be true. You have my brother riding on cloud nine, my grandfather in raptures over you, and your own father doing triple somersaults in his efforts to keep the whole romance running smoothly to the altar. You look at my brother with the kind of love that sets everyone sighing in ecstasy. Yet there, in the background, is Mark. Tall, and poetically handsome—as much your supposed type as my brother is. You spend hours holding hands over cups of coffee that never get drunk, and gaze into each other's eyes with the kind of look that puts that look of love for Daniel to shame.'

'H-he's a friend. Just a friend,' she insisted, trying to think, think quick and hard. She couldn't let Dane expose Mark, she just couldn't; it would ruin everything. 'H-he's been going through a bad time recently. A l-love-affair th-that's under stress. He——'

'And are you the other half of that stressed love-affair, Lily?'

'No!' she denied, instantly and hotly, but the betraying blush at the very idea made her out a liar, and Dane's mouth turned down into a sneer.

'I'm warning you,' he said grimly, 'I won't have my brother hurt. Daniel is too gullible and trusting for my taste, but it's what he is, and I will do anything—anything, got that?—to keep anyone from hurting him!'

'Then leave us alone!' she cried, wanting to add, And leave Mark alone too! But she didn't dare. The plea would reveal too much. 'Look...' She changed tack, trying desperately to make her brain function properly, but it wasn't easy. Despite the angry exchange they were having, Dane had not let go of her, and his closeness was having an intoxicating effect on her, churning her up inside so that she found it difficult to think of anything else. 'Daniel knows about Mark. He—he knows about our friendship and M-Mark's problems. He—he understands.'

'Well, I damned well don't,' he growled, 'just as I don't understand—this.'

His mouth swooped again, and this time there was no pretence at making it anything other than what it was. Dane kissed her with an angry determination to make her crumble. And she did, God help her. She felt herself splinter into a thousand tiny fragments of pure electric feeling, and when he muttered, 'You want me!' she could only groan in anguish and cling closer to him while he dragged his hand down between their bodies, untying the knots on their robes and tugging them apart. She cried out as the heat of his body melded with her own.

'I knew it!' he said triumphantly as he buried his hot mouth in the silken arch of her throat. 'I knew it from the first moment you let your eyes clash with mine that it was desire glowing there, not the dislike you pretend it is!'

'I hate you!' she whispered thickly, and meant it—still meant it because he'd made the last two years of her life hell when they could have been beautiful. He'd forced her to be aware of her own body's needs, of the tumult of sexual hunger that could grind the very tips of the nerves into stinging, aching pulp.

'Lily.'

She looked up, the ravages of her wretched flight into the past merging painfully with the present when she found herself staring up at Dane's hard, cutting face. And in sheer self-defence she lurched shakily to her feet.

'God in heaven,' he growled. 'Look at the state of you!'

The state of her. Numbly, she glanced down at herself, seeing for the first time her sheer black tights torn to tatters and exposing the grazes to her knees, her blouse, once a pretty white silk evening blouse, spattered with blood—Daniel's blood.

'Oh, God,' she choked, and swayed.

Something wrenched across Dane's face as he reached out and caught her to him, whatever antagonism he felt towards her laid aside by the utterly pathetic figure she made. She winced as his hands crushed her slender shoulders, and he drew back, a black frown darkening his taut white features.

'You're hurt!' he rasped. Then his eyes made a slashing scan of the small waiting-room and slewed to an accusing stop on the young nurse hovering uncertainly close by. 'Why hasn't she been attended to?' he demanded gratingly. 'Hell and damnation—do you only care for the dead here?'

As an outburst, it was appalling. It didn't take a lot to understand that he was responding to the shock of his brother's death. But the nurse jumped, startled, then bristled defensively. 'Mrs Norfolk wouldn't let anyone attend to her,' she explained stiffly.

Growling something not very nice beneath his breath, Dane thrust Lily back into the chair then squatted beside her so that he could study her more closely, his face whitening when he saw the dark bruise already causing an ugly swelling on the side of her face. Her left arm was hanging limply at her side, and another spurt of anger burst from him.

'What is this?' he demanded harshly. 'Why the hell haven't you let them see to you?'

'Daniel,' she murmured blankly. 'Daniel needed——'

'For God's sake!' The lid came off his temper. 'Daniel is dead, Lily. Dead! He doesn't need anyone's attention any more!'

'No——!' she cried, the denial tearing from her throat, and she wrenched back from him in the chair, staring at him through huge horror-filled eyes. 'No,' she choked. 'No!'

The nurse glared at him, then sat down beside Lily to place a protective arm around her. He grimaced, accepting that he deserved the look. He was behaving badly. Reaction. Reaction to a lot of things, but, if it hadn't been enough having to see his brother laid out in that cold, clean antiseptic room like that, finding Lily looking like this had been the limit, the utter bloody limit! She looked like an abused and bewildered child, left in the corner and forgotten about.

'Lily...' With effort he threaded some gentleness into his voice. She was trembling violently, her face buried in her hands. And it occurred to him at last that she hadn't taken the full truth of it all in as yet. Shock was holding it all back.

With grim intent, he pulled his own ragged emotions together and reached out to take her from the nurse. 'It's all right,' he told the young woman who was reluctant to let Lily go. 'I'll see to her. You just go and find someone who can look at her injuries. Lily...?' Gently he guided her head on to his shoulder.

The nurse left, and he knew, with a rueful irony, that she would be telling all and sundry out there what a cruel bastard that poor Mrs Norfolk's brother-in-law was.

She was right; he was a cruel bastard.

The tremors were abating, exhaustion making Lily settle more heavily against him, and after a few minutes Dane eased himself up and into the chair the nurse had just vacated, then carefully lifted Lily's chin so he could inspect the ugly bruising. It wasn't as bad as he'd first feared. And, Goddammit, any knock to this beautiful petal-fine skin would bruise it! Her mouth was cut too, one corner of it swollen as if someone had punched her. Clenching his teeth on the whip of angry violence that scored at him, he took out a handkerchief and gently cleaned the cut while she just sat there mutely complying with his ministrations. He didn't look directly into her eyes. He didn't dare. He had seen Lily in many guises, but never so weakened and vulnerable as she was right now.

He had never felt so bloody vulnerable himself. Daniel had been his only living relative. First his parents had gone, then Grandfather, and now—now Daniel.

'The arm,' he prompted huskily. 'Where does it hurt?'

'Shoulder,' she answered him. 'I wrenched my shoulder when Daniel——' She stopped, closing her eyes on the scene wanting to replay itself in her head. No, she told it desperately. No——

'Can you move it?'

Her eyes flicked open with a jerk, and she found herself looking straight into Dane's pale face. His mouth was tight, strain etching a thin white ring around its firmly moulded shape.

She nodded, lifting the arm and working it around in the shoulder socket, though it pained her to do it.

'Good—good,' he murmured. 'But I suppose we should get it X-rayed before we leave here——'

'No!' Lily cried. 'No. I don't want to be here any more.' A shudder ripped through her as she sent a hunted glance around the tiny waiting-room which had become her torture chamber for the last few hours. 'I w-want to go h-home now. Home...' Tears welled, and Dane sighed, taking her back into his arms.

'All right, Lily, all right. We'll go home just as soon as you think you can stand up.'

'Now,' she said instantly. And with what had to be a monumental effort on her part she straightened away from him and came shakily to her feet. 'I w-want to go now.'

Sighing, Dane joined her, automatically reaching out to fold her beneath his supporting arm. And they walked slowly, like two old people, across the waiting-room floor. At the door, she stopped, stiffening slightly against him.

'Sh-should I be signing something? D-doing something about—about Daniel?'

'No.' His voice sounded clipped and cold even to himself, but it hurt to even talk about all the formalities he'd had to go through before he'd been able to come for Lily. 'I've seen to it. Here.' Grimly he shifted the subject by removing his suit jacket and draping it around her shoulders. It wasn't until he watched her huddle gratefully into it that he realised she was cold. He hadn't given it to her for that reason, but to hide the state of her blood-splattered blouse from any curious people out there.

Daniel's blood, he realised suddenly, and almost gagged. 'Come on,' he said hoarsely. 'Let's get the hell out of here.'

Jo-Jo was hovering just outside the door, his thin, wiry frame restless as he paced up and down. Seeing them emerge, he came up to them. Dane glanced at him in surprise.

'I thought you might need me,' he explained his presence.

Dane nodded, silently grateful for the other man's thoughtfulness. 'Get the car round to the entrance, then.'

'It's already there.' The sheer cheek of him made Dane smile, albeit fleetingly. Then, drawing Lily more protectively beneath the curve of his arm, they started forward.

The casualty waiting-room was packed as they walked through. People looked up and stared at them, because it didn't take much to see a tragedy when you were that close to it. The nurse who had been with Lily when Dane arrived saw them and made a move as if to come over to them, then changed her mind when she saw the grim cast of Dane's face.

Coward, he thought as he led Lily out into the clear, warm night. And again the brief smile touched his bloodless lips.

The journey back to his apartment was achieved in silence. Once inside the big limousine with Jo-Jo ensconced behind the wheel, Lily seemed to turn right in on herself, huddling into Dane's coat in the far corner of the car and not moving again until they came to a stop and Dane was gently helping her out.

It wasn't until they were in the lift and speeding up to his fifth-floor apartment that Lily became aware of her surroundings. 'This is your place,' she said jerkily.

'Yes,' Dane quietly agreed to the obvious, adding nothing more.

'But I want to go home!'

'No.' Equally brief, he refused the demand. 'There's nothing there for you right now, Lily,' he said bluntly. 'You're staying with me.'

Nothing there. The words echoed hollowly in her head and she sank back listlessly against Dane's supporting arm, offering no more protests. Dane glanced at her, then at Jo-Jo, and gave a slight apologetic shrug for his blunt cruelty. The other man shrugged too, accepting the necessity for it. Even he could see that Mrs Norfolk was in a state of near-collapse.

The lift doors opened, and Jo-Jo left first, going to unlock the apartment door while Dane helped Lily. By the time they joined him just inside the hallway, Dane too could see the reason why the other man was standing stock-still in mute surprise.

'Well, well, well, if it isn't the wanderer returned,' drawled an acid-sweet gratingly sarcastic voice.

'I thought I told you to leave,' Dane said tightly.

'Did you, darling?' Judy shrugged her slender shoulders beneath the lush gold silk dress she had at last put back on. 'I didn't hear you.'

'You heard all right,' Dane snapped.

Lily looked up, the sound of that husky voice ringing a familiar bell in her fogged mind, just as Judy noticed her huddled into Dane's shoulder.

'Good God, Lily!' she exclaimed. 'What's happened to you? You look like you've just been run over by a bus!'

Lily blanched, then swayed. Dane cursed and caught her up in his arms just as her legs gave out beneath her. 'Get the hell out of here!' he barked at Judy.

'God, I'm sorry, boss!' Jo-Jo put in guiltily as Dane strode off down the hallway with Lily in his arms, almost knocking Judy over as he went by her. 'I'd forgotten all about——'

'Just see her off my property—right off!' Dane grated, and slammed the bedroom door shut in both horrified faces.

'Not nice of you, Dane,' Lily murmured as he lowered her on to the bed. 'Judy wasn't to know how closely she'd hit the nail on the head.'

'None of your damned business,' he snapped.

'True,' Lily conceded, then began to shiver violently. 'God, I'm so cold,' she whispered.

'Shock,' Dane diagnosed.

'We're both in shock,' Lily said, recognising his burst of anger for what it really was.

Dane glanced at her, his eyes still bright and hard with anger, then he grimaced. 'I'm shivering too,' he confided ruefully. 'Good grief, look at you, Lily,' he then added gruffly. 'She's right; you do look a state. What you need is a bath, those injuries attended to, then a warm bed and something strong to ease the shock.'

Unexpectedly, tears split her vision. 'I feel all used up,' she confessed.

'And no wonder.' He sighed, the sound raking his tension-locked chest as it left him. 'You've been through a harrowing experience. You're battered and bruised and totally exhausted.'

'Thank you,' she whispered. 'For bothering with me.'

'I would have to be ten kinds of a brute to be treating you like a leper just now.' Dane grimaced, well aware that she was referring to the fact that he'd spent the last two years treating her as though she were the lowest form of life on earth.

'But you usually are ten kinds of a brute,' she argued, lying curled on to her side still huddled in his jacket. He was sitting beside her, looking exhausted himself.

'But you're no leper, Lily,' Dane said sombrely. 'And you never have been.'

'I m-made him happy, you know. D-despite all those terrible things you believe about me, I did make Daniel happy.'

'I know you did.' He stood up jerkily. 'Get those clothes off if you can. I'll run you a bath.' And he disappeared into the adjoining bathroom before the pressure inside his chest exploded.

When he came back she was sitting on the edge of the bed, struggling with the sleeve of her blouse with her injured arm. He stood watching her for a few moments, then walked over to her, sighing as he squatted down beside her.

'Here,' he said. 'Let me.'

Gently, he eased the blouse away, then stilled, looking grimly at the dark bruising covering her shoulder. 'That's worse than I thought,' he muttered. 'Maybe I should have insisted you have it X-rayed.'

'No, it's just bruised,' she assured.

Aware of how much of her body was exposed to his gaze, she stood up, intending to slither past him and into the privacy of the bathroom before she attempted removing any more of her soiled and ragged clothes. But just the simple effort of standing on her own two feet had her swaying, and had Dane having to reach up to steady her.

He muttered something and came to his feet, maintaining a supportive grip on her uninjured arm as he did so. 'Damn you, Lily, do you have to make it so obvious that you hate my touch?'

'I don't.' Exhaustion made her honest. 'It just— isn't right for me to be here with you like this.'

'Because of what it led to the last time? Here, lean on me.' Gently he pulled her towards him until her cheek rested against the warmth of his shirt-front. And she hadn't the energy to stop him from undoing the clasp on her dark red silk skirt and drawing down the zip.

'No.' She shook her head. 'Because of who I am and who you are. It isn't right,' she repeated quietly.

'Step out of it.' His arm became supportive around her slender waist as she did as he bade and stepped out of the skirt. 'And who are you?' he challenged drily.

'Your brother's wife.'

'My dead brother's wife,' he corrected.

The cruelty of it sent a tremor rippling through her. 'Don't,' she whispered and looked pleadingly up at him through bright swimming eyes. 'Please don't, Dane. Not yet. I'm not ready to accept it yet. I . . .'

'And you think I want to?' he demanded, the glitter in his own eyes achingly suspicious. 'Stand still while I deal with this.' Grimly he undid the clip holding her skimpy bra in place. The next moment her breasts were pressing against the warmth of his chest and she had to hold her breath or groan at the sheer ecstasy of it. 'I saw him, Lily,' he murmured thickly. 'I saw him and I had to accept it!'

'Oh, God.' She began to shake, turning her face into his throat as the tears spilled over her eyes. 'I'm sorry. So sorry it had to be you.'

'Who else should it have been?' he questioned bleakly. 'I'm only glad it wasn't you who had to...' He stopped, his throat closing on a well of emotion. 'Come on,' he said gruffly. 'You're right, and it isn't the time for this. Let's get you into that bath and——'

'I can manage for myself now, thank you,' she told him primly.

'You think so?' Dane laughed huskily. 'Lily, you haven't a cat in hell's chance of making it to the bathroom door, never mind the bath itself, so cut out the shy virgin act when we both know it no longer applies, even if it did so once. And anyway, what you've got—beautiful though I know it to be—I've seen before. All of it,' he punctuated bluntly. 'Seeing it all again is going to be no revelation.'

With that, and while she came to terms with the dampening way he had put her in her place, Dane

picked her up again and carried her into the bathroom then silently and efficiently dealt with the rest
of her clothes before helping her sink into the waiting bath.

She sighed as the warm, soapy water folded
around her, closing her eyes and leaning back with
a feeling of intense relief.

'I'll leave you to it.'

She nodded her thanks, barely hearing him leave
the bathroom and quietly closing the door behind
him. Her body ached, her mind ached, the horrors
of the night crouching in the shadows, waiting to
leap on her the moment she weakened the grip she
was maintaining on her emotions.

How long she just lay there, floating in a half-
daze that shut out everything other than the warm,
soothing water, she didn't know, but the sound of
an impatient sigh brought her eyes flickering open
to find Dane back and standing over her, his expression rueful.

'Can't you do anything for yourself?' he mocked
drily.

'No,' she smiled, and closed her eyes again,
shutting him out as she was carefully shutting everything out, hoping he would just go away and
leave her alone.

Of course, he didn't. Dane had never done anything she wanted him to do. Instead he pulled up a
stool and sat down, then gently began to wash her.
As if she were a child, he washed her. And she let

him, simply because she did not have the energy to stop him—or the desire to.

'I never had you down as the nursemaid type,' she murmured into the steamy silence surrounding them.

'I never had me down as the type either,' he grimaced, then, quite out of the blue, 'What about Mark Radley—did you have them call him too?'

CHAPTER THREE

MARK!

Her eyes flew open, her breath catching in a ball of anguish in her throat as she sat up, dislodging Dane's hand from her body to stare starkly into the steam permeating around them.

'Oh, God,' she breathed. 'Mark!' How could she have forgotten all about Mark?

'I have to go out,' she gasped, standing up, energy-banks fully recharged from somewhere, so completely preoccupied that she didn't see Dane's face turn to hard granite.

'What?' he drawled. 'Like that?' sending his eyes sweeping cynically over her naked body coated in a layer of soap-silked water.

She blinked, sending her own eyes on the same journey his had just made, then blushed to the very roots of her hair, for the first time realising just how intimate she had allowed this situation to become. Her arms snapped up to wrap embarrassedly around herself, the action wrenching her bruised shoulder so that she winced.

'No. Not like this,' she whispered shakily, hating what those eyes did to her, how desperately alive they made her feel. 'I n-need a towel.'

She dragged her gaze away from him, and sent it on a hunted search of the steamy bathroom. It was awful. She was trembling, though not with shock any more, but because she was suddenly and stingingly aware of Dane as a man and not a sharer of grief. And as always when he looked at her like that her pulses began to throb, her breasts becoming heavy, the sensitive tips tingling as they nudged themselves into tight pink pearls of frustrated desire.

He smiled knowingly, coming slowly to his feet and using those eyes to wreak even more havoc as they lifted slowly, tauntingly with him. Hatred, he called this harsh flash of awareness that always sprung up inside her when he caught her off guard like this. 'Knowing how much I hate you turns you on, Lily,' he'd mocked cruelly once. 'And you can't do a damned thing about it, can you?'

'Don't touch me!' The fact that he was reaching out with a hand sent her mind into a flat spin of panic.

He laughed, the hard sound bringing her gaze flickering up to clash with his. It was then she saw it, the towel he was holding out to her, and she snatched at it, only to find that Dane was not letting go.

'Lily,' he taunted softly, 'I've just been touching you all over. So what's the difference now?'

Shame engulfed her. 'M-Mark needs me.' She threw the name at him out of sheer desperation, expecting and seeing the mockery leave his gaze to be replaced with the hard, cold glint of disgust. 'I must go to him.'

The towel became her property as Dane let go of it and spun his back to her. 'You're a bitch, Lily,' he said flatly. 'If you must go to your lover, then go. After all...' his head twisted on his shoulders so he could send her a last scathing look '...there's no Daniel to protest any more, is there? You can do what you damned well like!'

The bathroom door slammed shut behind him, leaving her standing shivering in the cooling bath of water. A few moments later came the sound of the bedroom door slamming, and she smiled miserably to herself. She'd most definitely won that round, but at the expense of the near-harmony she and Dane had achieved. Her eyes filled with bright, hot tears, mouth working on a wretchedness which came from somewhere she did not want to name.

Then she was wrapping the towel around her and stepping hurriedly out of the bath. Dane—the blight of her wretched life, she thought heavily. But it was Mark she had to think about now, Mark who needed her.

She dried herself quickly, wrapping the towel sarong-wise around her before rushing into the bedroom to find her clothes. Then came to a stop. Her eyes frantically searched the room. Nothing. Her clothes were gone. Not a single thing was left. No ruined blouse, no bra, shoes—with a twist that set her bruised face thumping, she spun around to look back into the bathroom. Even her panties and her ruined tights had gone. She hadn't seen Dane pick them up, but it could only be him who had removed them.

'Swine!' she choked, tears of angry frustration filling her eyes. 'Swine—swine!'

It took a few minutes to click, but eventually she remembered that Jo-Jo usually made sure there was a bathrobe hung up in every bathroom, and she rushed back in there, finding it hanging behind the door, and dragged it on.

The hallway was empty when she left the bedroom, the doors leading off it all closed. Setting her teeth, she walked quickly on bare feet on the cool, tiled surface to the lounge and threw open the door.

Dane was reclining in one of the several soft-cushioned armchairs, his dark head thrown back, eyes closed, a glass of what looked like brandy in his hand.

He looked exhausted. Utterly used up. And the knowledge that he too must be suffering the loss of Daniel cooled her anger somewhat as she padded over to stand in front of him.

'Dane,' she murmured tentatively. 'I need my clothes. Please, Dane!' she pleaded when he did not so much as flicker an eye. 'I have to go and see Mark!'

'Why? To celebrate your freedom from Daniel?'

It was a cruel accusation. But years of practice against Dane's cutting remarks helped her absorb them without retaliating much.

'Mark is Daniel's—best friend,' she stated quietly. 'It will devastate him if he hears the news from another source. It will be much kinder to him to hear it from me.'

'*Was* Daniel's best friend,' Dane corrected. 'He might have been a lousy kind of friend to my brother behind his back. But the word is *was* Lily, either way. Daniel is dead, remember.'

'God,' she choked, blanching at his bluntness. 'How can you be so cruel?'

'To you?' His eyes opened at last, hard as pebbles and icy cold. 'Easily. Until I mentioned the swine, you hadn't even thought of him. So what does that make you?'

A thoughtless, selfish bastard, she thought, and sank wearily into a chair. A hand went to her brow, trembling fingers stroking over the bruising at the side of her face. She winced, the area sore to the touch as well as making her head thump unbearably.

'You're exhausted,' Dane said grimly. 'You aren't fit to go anywhere.'

'I'm still going to see Mark,' she warned him stubbornly.

'Then I suggest you use the phone,' he drawled, and closed his eyes again in dismissal.

But Lily shook her head. The phone was no use. When Mark was working he simply unplugged it so he couldn't be disturbed. No, there was only one way of reaching him, and that was by going to his Chelsea home and letting herself in with her own key.

Chelsea ... A wave of nausea settled over her. It was only a few short hours ago that she and Daniel had left there after sharing a pleasant dinner with Mark at the tiny bistro they often ate at when they met up in London. Happy, laughing, they'd parted in the high street, Mark walking back to the house while she and Daniel went off in the other direction to where they had parked the car in a small side-street.

Then the car had come screaming round the corner. That mad, speeding——

She cut those thoughts off sharply, and forced herself to get up out of the chair. The few minutes' inactivity had stiffened her limbs and new aches piled themselves on top of old aches, making it sheer agony to move a muscle. 'If you won't return my clothes,' she muttered, 'then I'll call a taxi and go as I am.'

'You will?' His eyes came open with the sardonic lifting of those straight black brows. He flicked a glance up and down her. 'Lucky cabbie,' he drawled. 'It should make his night, taxiing you around looking like that.'

Giving up on the whole useless conversation, Lily sighed and spun away, making for the door. He could mock her all he damned well liked, but she would see Mark tonight if it killed——

Oh, God. She stopped. What a terrible thing to think! Daniel! Oh, Daniel, why did this have to happen now, when everything was about to come right? Swallowing on a fresh bank of tears, she forced her feet to move again, walking out of the lounge and down the hall to Dane's study. She was just lifting the telephone receiver to her ear when he appeared at the door.

'All right. I'll find you something to wear. Your own clothes are ruined, so it will have to be something else.' He sounded wearied to death with the whole affair. Looked it too, she noticed as she watched him turn and lope away.

Something cracked inside her. One of her carefully erected barriers against him coming crashing down, she recognised. The trouble with Dane was that he always had managed to reach her emotionally when she could best do without it. And just then, as he'd stood leaning heavily against the doorjamb, she'd felt her whole heart move in wretched sympathy with his drawn-faced, defeated stance.

Despite everything that Dane was that she despised she could not deny the fact that he'd loved his brother. Until she came along, they'd been close—very close, to hear Daniel tell it. Yet she frowned as she followed Dane down the hall and into his own bedroom, they could not have been that close or Dane would know and understand better the complicated relationship between herself, Daniel and Mark.

'Here.' He handed her a white T-shirt and a pair of stone-washed denims. 'They belong to Danny, so they shouldn't be too bad a fit.'

The 'Danny' had come out unknowingly, but hearing it on Dane's lips brought fresh tears to her eyes. Dane was the only person who had ever called Daniel by that name. 'Big brother's privilege,' Daniel had told her once. 'Let anyone else try it and I'll knock their block off.'

'He loved you, Dane,' she heard herself saying without really knowing why. The tears still blurred her vision as she looked up at him, mouth trembling as she added huskily, 'He was so proud of you. It hurt him that you couldn't accept me as his wife.'

'It wasn't you I couldn't accept, but your reasons for marrying him at all,' he said gruffly.

'I cared deeply for him—what more could any man ask for?'

'Faithfulness.'

'I was faithful to him!'

'No!' he growled, and suddenly he was furious again, his eyes flashing bitter sparks at her. 'You were unfaithful to Daniel every time you sat gazing into that other swine's eyes over your forgotten cups of coffee! You were unfaithful to him every time you looked at me with hunger in your eyes!' His mouth took on an ugly sneer. 'Where is the faith, Lily, in lusting after another man's body while you clung so *faithfully* to my brother's side? You can stick your kind of faith,' he derided thickly as he turned away from her. 'Don't you dare try telling me how much you loved my brother when I know it for the filthy lie it really is!'

She turned and ran. It was the only thing to do, or show Dane a complete breakdown of everything she held precious inside her. Tears aching for release, the dizzying see-saw sway of countless emotions rendering her virtually incapable of doing a thing for herself, she struggled into the borrowed shirt and jeans, her bruised shoulder nagging, head throbbing, and the desire—the desperate desire to just curl up and weep her heart out—gnawing like an animal on the blooded bones of her sanity.

No shoes, she realised. That meant going back to Dane to beg for them. Gritting her teeth, she all but crawled out of her bedroom—to find him waiting, standing stiff and grim just outside her door, her shoes dangling from one hand, the keys to his car dangling from the other.

His eyes raked over her, taking in the overlarge shirt tucked into the baggy waist of rolled-up jeans that seemed to be held up by will-power alone. She looked terrible, all wide-eyed and haunted, the bruising standing out against her pasty skin.

His jaw clenched. 'I'll take you wherever you want to go,' he muttered, dropping the shoes at her feet.

She bent to slip them on. 'I can easily call a——'

'No.' The refusal was curt and adamant. 'If you're determined to go out looking for your lover, then I'm coming with you.'

'Mark is not my lover.'

'You aren't fit to be out alone.' He ignored her denial. 'And after all I am responsible for you in a way—since you are my brother's widow and——'

She hit him then. Why it took that particular dig to make her react, when he'd uttered other far more inciting insults at her, she did not know, but referring to her as Daniel's widow had somehow made his death official, and it did something to her insides that made her temporarily lose control.

Without another word, she turned and walked up the hallway to the front door, not caring whether he followed or not. She'd had enough—more than enough of Dane's brand of sympathetic care to last her a lifetime.

He was right beside her in the lift. They didn't look at each other, yet Lily was intensely aware of his presence beside her, of the anger throbbing inside him, of his power, and the danger a man like Dane Norfolk presented when roused past all common bounds.

Had she pushed him that far? She pondered the point and found she didn't care about that either. She didn't care about anything any more but getting to Mark before the bad news got there before her.

The lift doors slid open and Lily walked out stiffly. Dane followed her, and they moved forward together, not touching, not speaking, but together. The limousine was parked where Jo-Jo had left it. Dane unlocked the door and saw her inside before going around the bonnet to climb in himself.

There was a moment's tense silence when she thought he was going to say something about her hitting him, then the engine fired and they were moving out into the plush, tree-lined street.

'Where?' he muttered.

She told him, giving an address only a few streets away from where the accident had taken place. Dane must have made the connection, because, grim-faced, he took the long way round, cutting down narrow side-streets and almost zig-zagging his way into Chelsea so they didn't have to pass by that particular spot.

He pulled up outside Mark's address, stopped the engine and made to get out.

'No.' Lily placed a hand on his arm to stop him. 'I'm going in there alone, Dane,' she said firmly. 'This has nothing to do with you, and I want to do it alone.'

'So you can both crow over my brother's misfortune?' he jeered. He was hitting out again, hurting her with the cruellest words he could think of.

'If you believe that,' she said quietly, 'then you certainly have no right to be included.'

His eyes narrowed on her, hard and suspicious. 'If you don't want me in there with you, Lily,' he countered, 'then it has to mean there are things going to be said you don't want me to hear.'

'That's right,' she nodded. 'Things that are none of your business.'

'Daniel is my business,' he claimed harshly.

'*Was*, Dane, *was*.' Coolly, she threw his own cruel words of earlier back in his face and watched him blanch as she had done. 'What goes on behind those walls is no one's business but mine and Mark's. Even Daniel has no say in it all any longer.'

'Perhaps the poor fool's relieved to be out of it,' he hit out gratingly.

'Perhaps he is at that,' Lily agreed, and somehow her agreement seemed to hold more sad, empty truth in it than Dane's deliberately provoking thrust had even tried to do. 'I won't be long,' she said, and got out of the car.

In actual fact, she was a hour. And when she eventually dragged herself out of Mark's house she was surprised to find Dane still waiting. She hadn't expected him to be, not after the exchange they'd had in the car. But she was glad—glad because she felt drained to the very dregs of her reserves, and it showed on her face as she climbed into the car and sat back, her head falling wearily on to the seat, eyes closed and deeply hollowed.

Dane sat studying her for a while, and she tensed, waiting for the expected volley of insinuations to come raking from his lips. It didn't come, and when he just leaned across her and silently fastened her seatbelt for her Lily allowed herself a quiet sigh of relief.

She'd had enough for one day—more than enough. It was time to think of Lily. And Lily needed to sleep—sleep until all the pain and grief had gone away...

Dane drew the car to a gentle halt and turned off the engine. Lily was asleep. No—he amended that. She was virtually comatose. Those incredible reserves of energy she had been running on had finally given out.

Sighing to himself, he stretched forward to lean his forearms against the steering-wheel, then rested his chin on them, staring sightlessly out at the dark summer night. This time yesterday, he'd been in New York, clinching a deal that gave him little satisfaction because of the ground he'd had to give to achieve success. He'd come home fed-up to his back teeth, with the only pleasure in the full month jetting the world the young filly he'd spotted going through its paces at a friend's ranch just outside Washington. He'd bought it, of course. And it was being shipped, as he sat here now, on its way to the stud, and to Daniel.

Daniel. A hot film of moisture shot across his eyes, and he sank his teeth into his resting forearm in an effort to contain the desire to cry, cry as he hadn't done since he was a baby—if he ever did then. He grimaced. To hear his mother tell it, he'd never cried—he brooded. A dark and determined child, with an ability to turn pain into aggression—the sharp, cutting, mental kind of aggression that made him assuage the pain by going right to its source and dealing with it—thoroughly.

Daniel had cried. Daniel had laughed. Daniel had filled their mother's heart with a love she had never got from her husband—or her first-born son, he grimly acknowledged. Oh, he'd loved her, but reservedly. His instincts, sharp even as a small boy, had warned him that if he let her his mother could have smothered him with that love. Just as she had tried to smother her husband and only succeeded in sending him scurrying for escape in the less demanding arms of other women.

Just as she had smothered Daniel.

Daniel. His face, laughing, the light summer breeze playing with his soft brown hair as he had sat easily on one of Grandfather's frisky mounts, mocking Dane because he'd just watched him see off one girlfriend with a kiss that lit flames around them, only to go straight back inside the house to get ready for a date with another girl. 'Love 'em and leave 'em, lover boy,' he'd teased him laughingly. 'But one day one of them will catch you out, and you'll be right up the creek without a paddle then.'

He'd grinned too, insolently—how old were they then? Daniel was about seventeen to his own twenty-three. 'But that's the excitement in the game, Danny. Not letting them catch you out. You ought to try it one day. You never know, you may find you enjoy the game, too.'

'Play with girls?' He'd almost fallen off the stallion in horror. 'No, thank you!' he'd drawled. 'I'll leave all that kind of thing to you—and Dad,' he'd added on a grimmer note. 'I'll stick to the gee-gees if you don't mind.'

'Oh, I don't mind.' Like Danny, he was aware that the humour had just seeped thoroughly out of the banter. But he'd tried to recapture the lighter mood. 'Less competition for me if you stay off the field.'

'I don't think you'll ever have any worries there, Dane,' Daniel had smiled, but the cloud had remained dark across his eyes as he said it. 'You'll always play in a different league than me.'

It turned out to be quite true. Daniel was what their mother had called 'a late developer'. If he was ever seen with girls over the next few years, then it was within a pack of both sexes. And even when he went off to university it was always a mixed bunch he went around with. No one girl he ever seemed to get serious over.

Until Sonia. Dane narrowed his eyes thoughtfully. That was the year Grandfather took ill, he recalled, and Dane's own workload had intensified when he took on his grandfather's role in the company. Sonia Cranston was Daniel's first real foray into the dangerous world of women and sex. Unlike the rest of his friends, Sonia did not belong to the university set. She was—on the face of it—nothing more than a leggy, fresh-faced stable-hand working for Grandfather at the stud. Dane was never quite sure just how deep their relationship had got before Daniel decided to put the brakes on it, but he had noticed on his brief visits down to Lefton over that long summer recess from university that his kid brother had acquired himself an adoring shadow. He remembered teasing Daniel about her.

'She's a pain in the neck,' Daniel had muttered. 'She—she thinks she's in love with me—won't leave me alone! She can't seem to understand that I'm not into—that.'

He could still see the dark heat of embarrassment crawl up his brother's attractive face. And he'd teased him about that, too. 'What?' he'd drawled. 'Not at all?'

The blush had deepened, and Dane remembered laughing at him. 'Oh, come on, Danny!' he'd mocked. 'She looks a cute little thing to me. Take some advice from your more experienced brother, and take what's on offer,' he'd advised. 'The practice will do you the world of good.'

He went abroad for several months just after that, and when he came back it was to find Sonia Cranston had left the stud, and a time-bomb behind her in the shape of their grandfather who was threatening to cut Daniel right out of his will. 'I can understand you boys wanting to play the field—did it myself when I was young. But I won't have you playing your games so close to home! A bloody stable-girl of all things!' he'd scoffed disgustedly. 'Your father may have disgraced the name of Norfolk with his playboy lifestyle, but even he knew better than to get involved with bloody paying staff!'

Daniel—a playboy? The very idea of it had made Dane want to laugh, but he hadn't dared because Grandfather was in full swing, and he'd have probably blown a blood vessel if he had.

But the idea that Daniel had taken his advice and at last tasted a bit of 'that' had pleased him no end—he'd been secretly beginning to wonder about his young brother.

'I'm telling you, Daniel,' Grandfather had raged on furiously, 'it's taken a long time for the Norfolk name to earn back its respect after what your father did to it, and I won't have you ruining that by playing around with the hired hands! So you find yourself a nice girl to settle down with, and prove to me that you're not going to follow in your father's footsteps—or you'll get nothing from me when I die!'

He meant the stud of course. Daniel's real passion. The only thing he had ever wanted out of the vast Norfolk empire.

So then came Lily.

Dane swivelled his head on his arm to look at her. She'd arrived so quickly on the heels of Sonia Cranston that Dane had suspected the relationship from the very beginning.

Yet, on the face of it, she suited Daniel. Pretty, fragile, slender, with that short, boyish crop of startlingly blonde hair she had never tried to grow any longer. And an air of innocence about her that had half fooled even him the first time he met her.

His mouth tightened—until he caught the way she looked at him. And there was nothing innocent in those brief, nervous glances. Nothing.

He sucked in a deep breath and let it out again. It hadn't helped that she'd tripped an answering chord inside himself—and she was nothing like the women he was usually attracted to. He liked his women tall, sleek, sophisticated, not resembling a saintly sprite from a child's storybook.

Yet kick his senses had, and had not stopped kicking at him since.

Twenty-two and the same age as Daniel. She had apparently been a member of his set for several years before she emerged from the midst as someone special.

'The boy shows good taste at last,' Grandfather had said with approval. 'And you could do worse than following his lead and find yourself a nice, meek, harmless thing like Lily.' Grandfather had fallen head over heels in love with Lily on first sight. 'She'll worship you till the day you die and keep the family name riding up there with the best.'

Harmless. The last thing he would call Lily was harmless as the aching twist he felt in his gut told him.

She stirred suddenly, as if sensing his attention on her, a frown spoiling the smoothness of her brow as a hand came up to touch the bruise on the side of her face. He watched her slender fingers caress the sore spot, press the swelling lightly, then fall limply back to her side. Then she sighed, the soft, whispering little sound lifting and dropping the full firmness of her breasts beneath the thin white T-shirt.

No bra, he noted grimly, watching the way the dusky corms of her nipples pressed against the thin cloth. He hadn't given her back her bra—or her panties, come to that. Why? He didn't know. Except that some nasty part of him liked the idea of her walking around wearing nothing but what he could see.

Had lover boy noticed the lack of underwear too? They had been alone in that house for an hour—long enough for him to not only notice, but touch—caress.

His mouth clenched as a dark, burning well of anger surged up inside him—a mark of his hatred for everything she stood for and a confusing, utterly contemptuous desire to be the only one in her life she could turn to for help and comfort. Hence the crazy swing of his emotions that had him cutting into her one moment and being prepared to do anything for her the next.

And she had turned to him, he reminded himself with a grim sense of triumph over lover boy Mark. Totally and unequivocally, it had been him she had wanted in her darkest hour. Him she had clung to. And if it hadn't been for his own stupid tongue, and a burning curiosity to know what had happened to Mark Radley while he'd been out of the country, she would not have given him a thought yet.

Mark Radley. One of the university set. The quiet one. The sensitive, arty, over-intense one. The one Dane hadn't seen brooding in the background of everything Daniel and Lily did until it was thrust on his notice by the bit of clever sleuthing he'd done.

His eyes narrowed thoughtfully. An odd little triangle. There was something about it that had never quite rung true. Too close to be normal— which didn't say much for Daniel for letting it go on.

Sighing, he straightened up in his seat, then looked at Lily again. He supposed he should wake her, yet for all the bitter emotions raging around inside him he found he didn't have the heart to do

it, and on another sigh he opened the car door and
climbed out into the balmy evening night, closing
the door with a quiet click before walking around
to her side and opening her door. She curled into his
arms as a trusting child would with its father, her
face burrowing into the warmth of his throat.

He grimaced as the soft puff of her breath sent
fine tingles running across his skin, then turned
towards the apartment block. The lift doors were
open and waiting. He walked inside and used his
elbow to work the console, then leant back against
the wall with Lily nestled against him.

Dane stared bleakly at the panelled ceiling of the
lift and didn't breathe—didn't breathe for a lot of
reasons, but mostly because having her wrapped
close to him like this was having its usual effect on
his senses. The feather-light weight of her, the soft,
feminine warmth of her, the silky brush of her hair
against his chin and the gentle heave of her breasts
against his——

He clenched his eyes tightly shut, despising himself, hating her.

The lift doors slid open, and he heaved a deep
breath and stepped out. Jo-Jo was waiting at the
apartment door. 'Saw you come in,' he explained
his vigilance.

Dane just nodded grimly and strode off down the
hall.

In her room, he laid her down on the bed then
stayed leaning over her to watch the way she curled

on to her side, the urge to brush his lips against her bruised cheek so powerful that his heart literally shook with need. She looked so defenceless lying there, childlike, innocent, vulnerable.

What a lie.

He jerked himself upright, his eyes black and hard as he went to flick the duvet over her, then paused, mouth tightening. He couldn't leave her to sleep like this. She was uncomfortable enough with all her cuts and bruises. The jeans at least would have to come off.

Clenching his jaw, he bent to unzip the jeans, slid them from beneath her hips then moved to her ankles to pull them free from her legs, then found himself standing there staring down at her as she lay there wearing nothing but the thin T-shirt. It covered her hips, but only just, the long, creamy line of her legs and thighs exposed to his hungry gaze while she slept on unaware.

'God!' Disgusted with himself, he flicked the duvet over her before turning away and walking out of the room.

CHAPTER FOUR

LILY was dreaming. She even knew it as a dream, though she seemed to have no control over what it made her see—and experience with that same blood-curdling horror.

'No,' she whimpered, trying to stop the events of the terrible night replaying themselves in her mind, as the car—that damned, murdering car—came hurtling out of the darkness towards them, so obviously out of control that it was clear it was going to hit something.

Something. That something was Daniel. 'No,' she whimpered again in an effort to block out the replay of the next horrific ten seconds. 'No—no—*no*!'

'Lily!' Strong hands took hold of her arms.

'Daniel!' she breathed—and tried to stop him hurling her to one side. Clutching at him. Trying to pull him with her, take him stumbling into safety with her.

But it just went on, playing it in her head exactly as it had happened. Daniel picking her up and throwing her to one side. Daniel turning, staring, watching with his eyes wide with knowledge as the car headlights honed on to him. Then the crashing, shuddering thump and that oddly passive grunt Daniel had given just before he'd disappeared in a tangle of broken, twisted metal.

'No!'

'Lily, for God's sake!'

A wheel hummed as it spun on its axle, the car lying upside-down. A door was wrenched open, scrambling hands pushing at it with all their might. Her own cry was wretched even to her own ears as she stumbled to her feet. Then a boy appeared—no older than a child to her stunned mind. He paused, she paused, and they stared at each other, blood pouring down his face from a cut high on his head. Then he was running, careering down the street like a drunk on the run, and Daniel—she couldn't even see Daniel in the mess the boy left behind.

The hands holding her issued a rough shake. Pain shot through her shoulder, and she came awake with the air rattling from her chest in short, panicky gasps, to find herself sitting bolt upright in the bed, staring into Dane's harsh face.

'Oh, God,' she panted, wilting within his grip, her body wet with sweat yet cold and shivering. 'Oh, God,' she repeated again.

'It was a dream,' Dane said harshly. 'Just a bad dream.'

'Yes.' She knew that. 'But oh, God, Dane,' she gasped. 'It's like a video tape, going over and over inside my head!'

'The accident?' The bed sank beside her as he sat down.

'Everything!' She began to shake violently. 'He shouldn't have pushed me out of the way like that! He sh-should have s-saved himself!'

'You can't blame yourself for Daniel's actions, Lily,' Dane said grimly.

Can't I? she thought despairingly. If Daniel hadn't paused to throw her aside, if he'd just leapt as his instincts must have told him to do—left her to rely on her own instincts, then maybe—maybe——

She shuddered, and Dane muttered something, pulling her closer to the solid warmth of his body. 'Dane,' she whispered wretchedly. 'Dane—Daniel is dead.'

It came then—the complete breakdown he had been expecting all evening. The one which would have come a whole lot sooner if her grief had not been diverted by worry for Mark Radley. And she began to cry, the sobs coming from so deep inside her that he was afraid she might choke on them.

Cursing softly to himself, he hooked an arm around her to drag her out from beneath the duvet and on to his lap, ruthlessly having to shut his mind off from the sting of heated pleasure he experienced as the T-shirt slid up her body, exposing more than was safe of her slender thighs. Swallowing tensely, he wrapped his arms around her while she sobbed.

'Oh, Dane,' she gasped.

'Don't,' he murmured, the emotion of it beginning to get to him too. And, because he needed to, he buried his face in her short, silky hair, searching for a comfort that—no matter how else he felt about Lily—only she could give him.

'Is she all right?'

Dane's head came up, his face revealing the ravages of his own emotions as he stared bleakly at Jo-Jo hovering in the doorway.

'Get me some brandy,' he rasped.

Jo-Jo nodded and disappeared, then came back seconds later with a bottle of his best cognac and a glass. 'Poor thing,' he murmured as he uncorked the bottle and poured a generous amount into the glass. 'She loved him a lot, didn't she?'

Did she? Dane declined to answer, accepting the glass Jo-Jo handed to him then dismissing him with his mouth tightly shut. She certainly felt something for Daniel to be as stricken as this. But love? He could not accept that. Mark Radley got in the way. Mark, and the way she always—always ended up responding to himself, even when he was being particularly cruel to her.

A woman in love did not lust after another man's body.

Ruthlessly, he tugged down her chin with his thumb and put the glass to her bloodless lips. She choked as the brandy seeped into her throat, then looked up at him through bright, accusing eyes.

'It stopped the hysterics, didn't it?' he drawled, raising a mocking eyebrow at her.

'One day I'll pay you back for all the cruel things you've done to me, Dane Norfolk,' she vowed hoarsely.

'I look forward to it,' he replied.

She opened her mouth to retaliate. But, suddenly weary of it all, Dane placed a finger over her lips to stop her.

'No more tonight, Lily,' he commanded grimly. 'You've had enough. I've had enough.'

'Yes,' she agreed, but the tears filled her eyes again. 'I saw him, Dane,' she whispered. 'I s-saw what that car did to him. How am I ever going to live with that, knowing he could have saved himself if he hadn't u-used precious seconds to get me out of the w-way?'

'For God's sake!' he groaned, the grief of it, the sheer bloody horror of it, making him push her back against the pillows and come down above her.

'But it's my fault he's dead!' she choked, and hit out at him wildly, guilt mirrored in the aching torment of her eyes.

'No.' He caught her flailing hands and drew them grimly to her sides. 'No, Lily,' he insisted. 'This is shock talking, and too much grief for your mind to cope with right now.' He lifted a finger to gently wipe away the tears spiking her dusky lashes. 'Just give yourself a little time,' he advised.

More tears replaced the ones he had just removed. He watched them brim with a dark fascination that had no root in their shared grief, then did what he had been dying to do the first time they'd appeared, and lowered his mouth to lick the fresh set of tears away.

He felt her sudden intake of air, her body stir beneath him in response to his being so intimate. In the last few hours he'd cradled her in his arms, stripped her, bathed her, and forced brandy down her lovely throat. He'd yelled at her, insulted her, felt the stinging slap of her hand across his face, yet nothing—none of the wild turmoil of emotions he'd felt through all of that—even remotely compared with what he was experiencing now as he lay there with her, tasting her tears on his tongue.

For two years he'd yearned to taste her again. Yearned for it the way an alcoholic did his next drink, knowing that it would act like poison on his system, knowing that it was utterly, totally forbidden. And like poison the taste of her tears ran through him, poisoning his will to draw back, let her go before it was too late and she killed every ounce of decency he had left in him.

'No, Dane.' She could see it in his eyes, the black, smouldering addict's fight with himself. And she was trembling again, though not with distress this

time, but with a fear that was intoxicatingly over-
laid with her own black passions. Her lashes no
longer spiked with tears but with the moisture from
his tongue, quivered above the tormented blue of
her eyes, her mouth was softly parted and still—still
because she didn't dare breathe in case she sent the
whole thing slipping dangerously over the edge. He
was suddenly aware of her warmth, her softness,
the knowledge that she wore nothing beneath the
thin covering of that T-shirt.

He dragged in a strangled breath as his heart began to thunder out a command older than time itself. One of his hands lay along her silken thigh, his
chest, heaving against the pressure building inside
his lungs, could feel the twin thrust of her aroused
breasts pressing into him. The T-shirt had ridden up
around her waist—a waist so slender and firm that
he was almost choking on the desire to span it with
his hands, caress her warm skin, feel her respond—respond to him as she had never responded to any man——

'God help me,' he breathed, and fought it—
fought it with everything he had in him while she
just lay there waiting to find out which part of him
won the battle, too weak with exhaustion and too
trapped by her own trauma of emotion to help him
at all.

They were both shaking, the air around them
throbbing with a high tensile stress which matched
the tensile throb of his heart. He clenched his teeth

together, stared angrily into her beautiful eyes, then down at her inviting mouth. Then with a raking grasp at his self-control he rolled away from her. And left the room.

Lily watched him disappear with her eyes wide and knowing. He had been going to kiss her then. And not because he was angry and wanted to punish her. Not because they were sharing a moment of mutual grief. But because he'd needed to. Needed to with a power that still burned like a flame inside them both.

Painfully, she closed her eyes. 'God, Daniel,' she whispered, 'what have I let him do to me?'

No answer came back from Daniel, because he was no longer there to help. But a small voice inside herself replied, thin and hollow, He's been doing it to you for two years. Why should you expect it to be different now?

There was a coolness between them the next day, brought on mainly by a defensive need to protect themselves from what kept on bubbling up between them.

'I need to get back to the stud,' Lily told Dane quietly. 'And I need to collect Dan——' she swallowed thickly '—Daniel's car from Chelsea.'

He glanced at her over the top of his morning paper, his silver-grey eyes giving nothing away. She was still in Daniel's clothes, her face beneath its cap of short blonde hair showing the ravages of strain.

'You aren't fit to be going anywhere,' he said, sliding his dispassionate gaze over her bruised cheek, which looked much worse this morning, then smiling grimly when she jerked a self-conscious hand up to cover the ugly blemish. 'An emotional and physical wreck. And the only thing you're going to be doing for the next few days is resting, and recharging your energy for the ordeal to come.'

Daniel's burial. She shivered, her slender figure seeming to cave in on itself in an effort to field the sharp thrust of pain.

'There's the funeral to arrange,' she whispered shakily. 'And—and I need some clothes. I . . .'

Her voice trailed off and Dane's mouth tightened. 'You're not stupid, Lily,' he drawled. 'You know as well as I do that any funeral arrangements can be made as easily from here as from the stud. I shall——'

'But Daniel would want to be buried in Lefton!' she cried, completely misunderstanding him.

'And so he shall,' Dane said patiently. 'But even you have to admit that I am more qualified than you to make those arrangements. I have had a lot of practice at it over the last few years after all.' First his father over five years ago now, followed quickly by his mother. Then Grandfather only six months ago—— He sucked in a tight breath and grimly folded his newspaper. 'But I can't leave

London at present,' he went on. 'And you aren't fit to manage the drive down to the stud, so——'

'I don't want to stay here,' she cut in huskily.

Anger flared up inside him. 'Well, you've got no bloody choice!' he snapped, making her wince. Tensely, he came to his feet, hooking his jacket from the back of a spare chair. 'Do you think I didn't notice the way you walked in here this morning?' he muttered. 'You could barely put one foot in front of the other, your muscles have stiffened up so much! So stop trying to behave like the very independent widow I have no doubt you are going to be, and let me do the arranging and you do the grieving—at least until Daniel is buried!'

'God, you're a cruel bastard,' she choked.

'Perhaps,' he conceded. 'But, you see, I remember Mark Radley, and how you ran helter-skelter into his arms at the first chance you could get. So maybe I have a right to be cruel to you—on my dead brother's behalf.'

But she hadn't run straight to Mark, Lily argued silently. She'd run straight to Dane. Him—— Her eyes did a malevolent scan of his lean, hard body encased in its smart city suit. Her real tormentor in life. The persecutor of all her sins.

'I still need clothes,' she reminded him.

Dane nodded, already moving towards the breakfast-room door as if he couldn't get away from her fast enough. 'And Jo-Jo will drive down to the stud this morning and collect them for you,' he agreed. 'But you, Lily——' suddenly he was swinging back to face her, his eyes hard with threat '—will stay here. I don't want you getting Jo-Jo into trouble by trying to talk him into taking you too—and I don't want you talking to Radley on my telephone the moment both Jo-Jo and I are out of here!' he added harshly. 'The man has received the bad news, now he can deal with it in his own way—but without the help of my brother's brand new widow!'

'Oh—get out!' she choked, sick of him and his insinuations. 'Go on——' She waved a danger-ously dismissive hand at him. 'Go and do what you're so good at doing, Dane, and earn another million or two while you fit in grieving for your brother between lulls in the damned stock mar-ket!'

He breathed something utterly disgraceful, his shoulders bracing against the hellish fall-out of bitterness permeating the whole sunny room. Then he sighed raspingly and thrust a hand through his sleekly brushed hair—sleek like the rest of him, Lily noted helplessly, sleek, honed, sharp, smooth.

Mouth going dry, she looked away, down at the coffee-cup steaming in front of her. A silence fell, taut but oddly heavy with it. Lily picked up a spoon and began stirring absently at the coffee while Dane remained where he was by the door, clearly trying to grab some control over himself.

Something they both needed to do, Lily acknowledged with a wry tilt to her mouth—in more ways than just the terrible antipathy that leapt so quickly between them.

'I'll be back for lunch,' Dane said eventually, his voice gruff and tight. 'Make a list of all the things you require from the stud, and give it to Jo-Jo.'

Then he walked away, while Lily sat, listening to the aggressive tap of his shoes on the black and white tiled hall floor, wishing she could understand why tears were trickling down her cheeks.

You're crying too much, she told herself, and firmly wiped the tears away. Tears wouldn't bring Daniel back. Tears wouldn't stop Dane despising her as much as he did. Wearily, she got up from the table, wincing as just about every muscle she possessed protested at the exercise.

There were things she had to do. Despite Dane's insistence that he see to it all, she had calls to make, people who deserved to hear the bad news before the announcement appeared in the papers. Friends—colleagues of Daniel's. And her own parents, she reminded herself heavily.

Calculating the time-difference, she decided to ring her parents as soon as Dane left. She was reluctant to interrupt their long stay in Australia where her father had taken her mother to convalesce in the kinder weather after a long-term illness which was at last under control. It didn't seem fair to spoil their pleasure with such bad news. But the knowledge that an announcement would appear in the papers tomorrow made it essential that she break the news to them first.

Her mother wept, and Lily had to steel herself not to join in. 'You need me,' she sobbed. 'We're coming home.'

'No!' Lily protested. 'No, Mother, listen to me. I don't want you rushing back here making yourself ill all over again! I'm staying with Dane,' she explained quickly, 'and between us we're—coping.'

'Dane will take good care of you.' Her mother's tears eased a little. She, like most women, was not immune to Dane's air of strength and magnetic charm. She approved of the arrangement—as Lily had known she would do. 'Poor boy,' she sniffed. 'He has no one left now, does he? No family at all, except you, Lily.'

'Yes, he has me,' she huskily agreed, but wondered wryly what Dane would have to say to that loaded remark. 'And I have him,' she added sturdily. 'It's—easier for both of us this way.'

And, oddly, Lily recognised a faint grain of truth to that. Though why it was there she had no idea, since they'd done hardly anything else but insult each other from the moment they'd come into contact!

'Oh, dear,' her mother murmured as the tears began falling again. 'I shall have to pass you to your father...'

'She's gone for a weep,' a gruff voice said a few seconds later. 'Hello, sweetheart,' her father greeted heavily. 'I'm so sorry, Lily. Life's so damned unfair, isn't it? Poor Daniel.'

'Yes,' she whispered.

'That boy was more to me than just my son-in-law,' he murmured. 'He was my saviour, too. I'm going to miss him.'

'I know.' Tears split her eyes. She was well aware of how much her father owed to Daniel.

'H-how are you holding up?' he asked.

'I'm—coping.' She gave him the same answer she had given her mother, and wondered grimly to herself how many more times she would be repeating that phrase over the next few days.

'If you need us for anything—anything at all, then you mustn't hesitate to tell us. We can be over there in no time and...'

'It's better you don't,' she told him. 'I—I can handle it better without——' Mother weeping all over me, she had been going to say, but changed it quickly to, 'On my own.'

But he understood. 'She's still a little too emotional just now,' he agreed. Her illness had left her like that—too vulnerable to her feelings for her own good. 'But you know we love you, Lily, and we'll be thinking of you.'

'Yes,' she said again, her own voice thickening in weak yearning for a bit of that love right now. 'Thank you, and I love you too.'

'Then take care, sweetheart. And offer our sincere regrets to Dane also.'

She nodded. 'I will,' she assured him.

She replaced the receiver then laid her arms on Dane's desk so that she could rest her face on it.

'Very touching,' a cold voice said from the doorway.

Her head came up sharply, eyes widening in surprise when she found Dane standing in the doorway, a hand still grasping the doorknob, his expression contemptuous.

'Lover boy I presume,' he drawled.

Lily stiffened instantly. 'My father, actually,' she clipped, and watched the anger leave his face only to feel it well up inside herself. She was sick of him always thinking the worst of her. 'I presume you need this room and I'm intruding?' Standing up, she walked stiffly towards him. 'I'll come back to finish my calls later——'

'Lily——' Dane caught her arm as she went to stalk by him. 'I'm—sorry.'

'Are you?' Her eyes flashed icy blue sparks at him.

He grimaced ruefully. 'I came back because I'd forgotten some papers I needed, and hearing you—saying what you did—obviously made me think of——' He shrugged and went silent, seeing that he wasn't solving things any. 'Stay and make your phone calls,' he invited. 'I shall be thirty seconds, no more.'

Letting go of her arm, he walked over to his desk and unlocked a drawer. Lily hovered, still angry, yet aware that she really had no right to be. Dane had a right to be suspicious of her. She was the deceitful one, not him.

'How are your parents?' he asked after a moment. He had his back to her, his lean fingers flicking through a sheaf of documents. 'How have they taken the news?'

'They're upset, naturally,' she said, hating the way she couldn't take her eyes off him. Even with his back to her, his aggressive brand of masculinity still had the ability to reach out to her. With an effort she made herself answer him normally. 'Th-they're in Australia at the moment. Daddy took my mother there to convalesce.'

He turned at that, his eyes darkened by remorse. 'I'm sorry,' he said again. 'I'd forgotten all about your mother's illness.' Sighing, he put down the papers, then ran an impatient hand through his hair. 'I'm not very thoughtful where you're concerned, am I?' he grimaced.

'You're thoughtful enough,' she mumbled, uncomfortable now she'd made him feel guilty. He hadn't been that far from the truth with his initial accusation. If he'd arrived a few minutes later, he would have caught her talking to Mark. And God knew what he'd have overheard then. 'It can't be easy for you having me here when you so actively dislike me.'

'Dislike?' he questioned drily. 'I don't ever recall saying I "disliked" you.'

'Hate, then.' She gave a what's-the-difference shrug, her eyes unknowingly bleak. 'I was just trying to let you know that I appreciate your—kindness.'

'Kindness?' Those black bars for brows rose upwards, a sardonic attitude replacing the remorse. 'I don't think you and I must be living on the same wavelength, Lily, if you can interpret so much as an inch of kindness in anything I've said or done.'

'Duty, then!' she flashed impatiently. 'What does it matter? I was only trying to thank you the way any grateful guest would!'

'Ah,' he drawled, still mocking her. 'Now your gratitude I will accept. You should be grateful that I didn't give you the good hiding you deserved for smacking me across the face last night. And the only thing that saved you,' he informed her at her suddenly defiant expression, 'was the fact that that poor body of yours is wearing enough bruises already.'

Her hand jerked up automatically to cover the purple swelling on her face. 'Quite,' drawled Dane. 'Now, come back here,' he commanded.

She didn't move. 'What for?' she asked suspiciously.

'I have something for you,' he explained.

But she didn't trust the sudden glint in his eyes. 'What?' she demanded.

'Your address book,' he said innocently, and held the little black book out to her.

Lily stared at it, then moved slowly towards his outstretched hand. As she reached for the book, Dane deftly lifted his other hand and caught her around her waist.

'Oh!' she gasped. 'What do you think you're doing?'

'Being kind,' he mocked as he moved backwards to lean against the desk, taking her with him. Then suddenly he was serious, the silver flecks in his eyes which made them look so cold most of the time darkening to grey, giving them an odd kind of gentleness that made her heart squeeze. 'You were feeling rotten when I came in, and I attacked you for it. I'm sorry.'

'Y-you've already told me so twice,' she dismissed, lowering her eyes from his because she was acutely aware that she was making no effort to pull away from him as she should. And Dane had to be aware of that, too.

'I know, but I want you to know I meant it.'

'I do know.'

'No, you don't,' he denied. 'You'll never know just how sorry I am, Lily, that things could not be different between us.'

'Dane—please——!' Weak tears spurted back into her eyes and she glanced at him pleadingly. 'Please don't be nice to me!' she choked. 'It only makes it worse! I——'

'What worse, Lily?' he questioned. 'This?' And lowered his mouth down on to hers.

Of course it was 'this', she acknowledged miserably as he swung her away on the kind of embrace she had hungered after for years. It was 'this' that kept the tension buzzing like static around them every time they were in the same room! 'This' that had made it so difficult for them to part last night without 'this' happening. And 'this' that had made the last two years of her life hell, wanting, needing, and knowing that it could never be. It was 'this' that had, in the end, driven her to beg Daniel to set her free, set them all free so that they could be whole and clean again, instead of coloured by the taint of a deception that should never have been allowed to start in the first place.

They were both having trouble breathing when eventually their mouths broke apart. 'Now,' he murmured, allowing his lips to linger close to hers as he spoke. 'That wasn't nice of me at all, was it? Kissing my brother's widow before he's been gone barely a day.' She broke the contact, jerking her head back to glare her hatred at him. He smiled, but it was full of cruel mockery. 'Does that get rid of all those other softer descriptions you felt you should apply to me too, like kind, and compassionate, now that I've reminded you what a nasty rat I really am?'

She didn't answer him—couldn't. Her throat was too tightly locked by guilt and shame. He had mentioned Daniel, but she knew that if he hadn't she would not have given him a thought. Not a single thought.

Dane gently but pointedly pushed her away from him, and straightened up, turning to put down her address book and gather up his papers again.

'Why?' she burst out as he moved towards the door. 'Why do you persist in tormenting me like this?'

'You torment yourself, Lily,' he threw back coolly. 'Every time you look at me with hunger in your eyes, you're tormented. I'm just bastard enough to enjoy tasting what's on offer, that's all.'

' "Bastard", just about says it,' she retorted through the self-disgust his words inflicted.

Pausing at the door, he glanced back at her. His eyes were hard again, and cruelly taunting. 'Better than kind?' he posed. 'Better than compassionate?'

She turned away from him, and felt his soft mocking laughter shudder down her spine before the door closed quietly behind him. He hated her. Why it hurt so much when she'd always known he did she didn't understand. Tears. Tears which came too easily just now trickled slowly down her cheeks. She sniffed, and wiped them away with the back of her hand—a hand that could still feel the warmth of his body against its tingling palm.

CHAPTER FIVE

LILY made a few more phone calls, to close friends of hers and Daniel's mainly, who had the tears falling again. Then, setting her mouth and her composure because she knew she was going to need all the control she had in her for this next call, she picked up the phone and called Mark's number.

There was no reply, and that worried her. She let it ring and ring in the hope that he was there and just refusing to answer. The phone was plugged in. She knew it because she had done the job herself and made him promise not to unplug it again in case she needed to contact him. But if he was in the house her persistence did not coax him to pick up the phone and in the end she gave up. Sighing worriedly, she made a mental note to keep on trying at intervals and turned her attention to the list of things she required Jo-Jo to collect for her from the stud.

He took the list from her and smiled his thanks. 'Good,' he said. 'I can ring it through to your housekeeper so she can have it all ready for the boss to collect.'

'But——' she frowned at him. 'I thought Dane said you were going.'

He looked at her through those sharp eyes of his. 'Have you looked in a mirror this morning, Mrs Norfolk?' he enquired gently. 'The boss was right when he decided you shouldn't be left on your own. You look shocking.'

Dane had decided that? When? she wondered. Before he gave her a lesson in humiliation or afterwards? What was it with him that he could toss her around like a cruel cat playing with a helpless mouse one moment, then be showing genuine concern for her the next? A pale hand crept up to stroke gently at the nagging ache in her head beneath the bruise, confusion and the constant desire to weep tightening the frown on her brow.

'Why don't you go back to bed,' Jo-Jo suggested, 'and just leave everything to the boss and me?'

'Yes,' she whispered. 'I think I'll do that.'

But she tried Mark's number once more before she went. There was still no answer, and she took that worry with her to bed, and into the sleep she sank wearily into, waking late in the afternoon with Mark still in the forefront of her thoughts.

Trying his number again drew the same results, and the knowledge that he was distressed enough to do something stupid had her having to fight the urge to go around to the house and check it out. But the fear of Dane discovering where she'd gone was a big enough deterrent. She knew she wasn't fit for another bout of his bitter accusations. He might get angry enough to go around and face Mark with his suspicions.

And Mark, she knew for sure, was not up to Dane's brand of interrogation. He would cave in and tell him everything—if only to justify his own right to grieve.

No, she decided. It wasn't worth the risk. Mark was going to have to get himself through this on his own. She could help him no more. And, she mused thoughtfully, perhaps he knew that too, and that was why he wasn't answering her calls? She hoped so, she sincerely hoped so. For all their sakes, but most of all for Daniel's sake.

It was too late to drag the dirt now.

Still, she tried the number right into the late evening. And eventually went to bed having had no success in reaching him.

Her case had arrived by special messenger during the afternoon, sent there by Dane who had apparently driven straight back to his office after going to the stud. Pressure of work, he'd told Jo-Jo over the phone. But Lily knew that it was the pressure they generated between the two of them that kept him away. So she was glad of the respite. They'd always been able to spark each other off easily enough, but the added stress of Daniel's death, coupled with their being thrown together like this, had made the friction between them fifty times worse.

But it was a relief to have her own things about her. After showering the stresses of the day away, she slipped into the nightdress Mrs Jakes, her housekeeper, had sent, and crawled beneath the duvet wondering where Dane had got to. Ten o'clock in the evening, and still he had not shown his face. What kind of business pressure could it be to keep him working when he should be grieving for his brother? she wondered.

Or perhaps it wasn't business at all, she then thought pettishly. It was more likely that he'd gone in search of comfort from one of his women.

And why not? she demanded of the hot shaft of jealousy that thought hit her with. He was foot-loose and fancy-free. He could find his comfort wherever he liked! And Judy Mason had to be any man's idea of comfort. She was beautiful, she was sexy, she probably knew more ways than most to give a man comfort—and she was available—more than available if her presence here the night before was any indication. And perhaps he'd gone to make his peace with her after the way he'd had her thrown out the night before. And, knowing Judy's reputation, it should take all night.

All night, with Dane in her arms. Dane kissing her, loving her—— Lily buried her face into the pillow, hating herself for what she was, what she had allowed herself to become: a woman who lived a lie. She was a mass of them, she admitted bitterly. A big, bubbling cauldron of bad, scheming lies!

He was at the breakfast table when she walked in the next morning, though. Lily had not heard him return and she'd lain awake until deep into the night, so she could only assume that he had come back early this morning.

Quenching the desire to demand to know just where he had been last night, she sent him a cool smile instead. He did not return it, and on an inner sigh she recognised the look in his eyes as he ran them briefly over her before flicking them back to the paper he had spread out in front of him. Dane had reverted back to the normal grim-faced, cold-eyed stranger she was used to seeing.

'You received your things, I see,' he remarked.

'Yes—thank you.' She ran a nervous hand over the collar of her simple white blouse, then dropped it to the equally simple dark blue pleated skirt she was wearing.

He just shrugged her gratitude away, seemingly engrossed in the article he was studying in the newspaper. Lily poured herself a cup of coffee then sat sipping at it in silence, his attitude telling her that he did not want to make conversation, light or otherwise.

He was dressed for the City, she noted, in one of his dark pin-striped suits that so increased his air of

charge and power. And he'd only recently showered and shaved—his hair was still damp, lying
slickly in its expensive cut to his well shaped head,
his solid chin smooth and shiny, the skin still
showing the ravages of loss in its unusually sallow
pallor.

He glanced up, caught her looking at him, and
Lily flushed, glancing quickly down at her coffee-
cup. Those eyes could be so damned cold! Yet she
also knew how hot with passion they could become. Black, with hungry fires burning deep—deep
down inside——

'I've made all the necessary arrangements.' His
voice, as cold as his eyes, made her jerk to attention. 'The funeral will take place on Friday. I've left
your housekeeper, Mrs Jakes, to organise a light
lunch for those who will want to come back to the
stud afterwards. So there's no reason why we
should need to travel down there until Friday
morning. The funeral train will leave from there.'

Lily nodded, accepting his arrangements without argument. If she was truthful with herself, she
was relieved he had taken the awful job from her.

'Also,' he went on coolly, 'Mrs Jakes informed
me yesterday that she could find nothing—suitable
for you to wear for the funeral.'

Black, he meant. She had nothing in black.
Daniel had not liked seeing her dressed in black.
'It's a morbid colour, Lily. It reminds me of funer-
als. It makes me miserable to see you in it.'

She shuddered.

'So you'd better go out and buy yourself something,' Dane suggested as he got up from the table. 'I'll leave you Jo-Jo again. He'll drive you wherever you want to go.' He slid his hand inside his jacket and withdrew a fine leather wallet. 'Here,' he said, dropping a thick wad of notes on to the table. 'Use that to——'

'No!' Lily came shooting to her feet, the subdued mood his cool manner had put her in fleeing in the sight of this gross insult. 'I'll pay for anything I buy myself!' she told him furiously. 'So just put your money away!'

He arched an eyebrow at her outburst. 'You mean you'll pay for it with Daniel's money, don't you?' he drawled.

She flushed, not with guilt but with anger. 'My own money!' she corrected. 'Daniel may have been a whiz with horses, Dane, but you know perfectly well it was me who kept the place running as a viable business—and got paid a respectable wage for doing so! I'll pay for my own clothes.' Angrily she shoved the wad of money back at him. 'And don't you dare to denigrate me like that again!'

He watched her for a moment, his expression telling her nothing while hers told him everything from every seething part of her. Then he nodded his dark head. 'Fine,' he said, and scooped up the money before turning and walking to the door. 'By the way,' he murmured as he reached it, 'I found

Radley at the stud when I arrived there yesterday. He was clearing his belongings out of his room.'

Alarm ricocheted like lightning through her, and she had to fight to keep her expression under control as she turned to look at him. 'W-what did you say to him?' Something about the satisfied tilt to his mouth told her he hadn't let Mark alone in his grief.

Dane shrugged those elegant shoulders of his, tossing Mark aside as if he didn't matter. 'I—thanked him for his tact,' he drawled smoothly. 'After all, he does seem to have realised how bad it looked, him living there as your lover under the same roof as your husband—even if it did come too late to save Daniel's feelings.'

The door closed quietly behind him, and Lily sank into her chair, relief working with an aching helplessness that made her feel utterly weakened inside. He'd seen and understood nothing, as always, blind to what he did not want to see.

At least she now knew where Mark had been yesterday—though the idea that he'd come up against Dane did nothing to ease her mind. Oh, Daniel, she thought heavily, poor Mark. Poor lost and wretched Mark.

The little church in Lefton village was packed. People from all over the area had come to pay their last respects to Daniel Norfolk, people who had known the Norfolk family for years, people who had either worked for or with the Norfolks at some point in their life. The Norfolks had been big land-owners here once upon a time—until as recently as when Dane's mother's death had come so soon after the husband whom she had loved totally, no matter how deeply he scarred that love with his many affairs.

Grandfather was buried here. And, if the fates played fair, really that should have been the last death the family should have experienced for a long time. But the fates rarely ever played fair. And once again the Norfolks were having to bury one of their loved ones.

Daniel's coffin looked lonely standing there before the altar, even heavily skirted in wreaths of flowers as it was. Lily trembled and moved closer to Dane, instinctively searching for comfort from the person closest to her. His arm accommodated her, tense but there, not withdrawn. For all he felt against her, he had not withdrawn his support at the final hour.

'All right?' he enquired.

She nodded, swallowing, glad of the wide-brimmed black hat she was wearing which hid her face from view.

'Hold on a little longer,' he murmured encouragingly—and surprised her by reaching out to take one of her cold hands in his.

For some reason, this simple gesture of concern hit her harder than everything else. The never-far-away tears filled her eyes once again as the minister began the solemn service. 'We have gathered here in the sight of God to say our farewell to...'

It was Dane she leaned on when they filed out of the church. Him she trusted to guide her away from the graveside afterwards and into the limousine waiting to take them back to the stud.

Once there, she climbed out of the car unaided, then stood looking up at the house with sad, empty eyes while she waited for Dane to join her.

The stud. Everyone referred to the rambling old place with its beautiful ivy strewn walls as the stud, but really it was Lefton Grange—the place where Daniel's grandfather had built up a healthy going concern from a hobby which took him away from the cut-throat pressure of high finance.

He'd loved this place, that sweet, grumpy old man. And so had Daniel.

Turning slowly, she gazed out over the rolling pastureland where, several times a day, you would see a line of horses taking their daily exercise with their whippet-sized grooms balanced precariously on their backs. There was no sign just now, though. The fields in front of her were empty. As empty as she was feeling inside.

Well, Daniel, she asked him silently, was it all worth it?

No answer came back. She hadn't expected it to. Daniel was gone, and with him he had taken the sense in the last two years.

Dane's hand, light on her arm, prompted her into moving forward. Jo-Jo was waiting for them at the drawing-room door.

'Here,' he said, 'drink this.' And offered them a sherry glass each, winking at Dane as he moved away. The other man grimaced and sipped, then watched steadily as Lily did the same.

'Good grief!' she coughed. 'What is it?'

'Your favourite bedtime drink,' Dane drawled.

'Brandy.' She shuddered, recognising the awful taste. 'For everyone?' she then asked curiously.

'No, just those people who are going to need it. So drink up, Lily,' he commanded grimly, letting his glance flicker around the steadily filling room. 'We have a couple more ordeals to get through yet, I'm afraid.'

He meant the reading of the will, of course, and this—the expected buffet wake. And an ordeal it was, to mingle with all these people when she wanted to just run and hide herself away somewhere. Yet once again it was Dane who propped her up, kept her going, moving with her from group to group, thanking them for their kindness in coming and accepting their sympathies in return.

She thought she would suffocate on the tension locked in her body by the time they began to filter away. And at last she felt she could excuse herself and go upstairs, grab a few moments alone to freshen up and ready herself for what was still to come: the reading of the will.

She had half expected to see Mark appear at some point during the funeral. But he hadn't. Sighing, she took herself over to the window to stare bleakly out, wondering worriedly where he was and what he was doing.

He should have come. No matter how badly he was feeling in himself, he should have come to Daniel's funeral, if only to make his peace with the man he——

Swallowing, she turned back to the room to find Dane standing in her doorway. Her heart stuttered then fell back into the dull, aching throb it had been maintaining all day. Dane was beginning to feel like her Nemesis, always just one step behind her as if waiting for her to stumble and fall.

She wouldn't, though, she told herself flatly. She had come too far and lasted too long to collapse now.

'Time?' she asked.

He nodded. 'Mr Trent is waiting for us in the study.'

'I . . .' She lowered her eyes from his, wanting to cry all over again, though not for Daniel—or even Mark this time—but for herself. She loved this man so! 'Just give me a moment . . .' she whispered, moving towards her dressing-table, ostensibly to run a comb through her hair; but really it was just an excuse to gather her ragged senses together before she felt fit to face him again.

'This is your room?'

'What?' The question surprised her into glancing at him. 'Oh, yes.' She let her eyes drift around the room which had been home to her for the last two years. 'Not very fashionable, I grant you,' she acknowledged his disapproving frown. 'But then this old house wasn't built for light modern furniture.'

'I wasn't thinking of that,' he said. 'It just surprises me, that's all, that you and Daniel should choose this room, when the three larger ones at the front are far more suitable for two people to share.'

Oh. Lily turned back to the mirror. It had never occurred to her that he would question the sleeping arrangements of the house. Now she sank her teeth into her bottom lip and wondered how she should answer him.

Dane used to be a regular weekend visitor to the stud before Daniel married her, but he had never stayed the night here since. So he wouldn't know that——

'I mean, Daniel's old room was only next door to this. So if you preferred the back view, why didn't you simply stay in there?'

'I liked this room better,' she murmured flatly.

'That's why Radley had taken over Daniel's?'

Mark's room? Lily frowned, stumped for an answer. What had given him that idea?

'Was he good with the horses, too?'

'Who, Mark?' She blinked, having to pull herself together, glad Dane hadn't insisted on a reply to the other question, because she literally didn't have one. 'He had to be, or he would not have been able to paint them as beautifully as he did.'

Mark was an artist, a man whose gift had brought him a reasonable living, since the wealthy owners of the racing horses stabled here were more than happy to pay him a handsome fee to capture their pricey investments in oils.

'He didn't come to the funeral,' Dane inserted quietly.

'I know.' Lily lowered the comb to stare at her own reflection, concern for Mark clouding her eyes once again.

'Guilty conscience, I suppose...'

'Or consideration for you!' she instantly flared in Mark's defence, spinning back to face him. 'You wouldn't have liked it if he had turned up today!'

'True,' he acknowledged. 'Which doesn't automatically follow that he had to stay away,' he then pointed out, implying that Mark was a coward—which, Lily heavily conceded, he probably was. 'He could at least have been here to support you.' Lily pressed her lips together and refused to answer that one. 'And I do believe he is mentioned in Daniel's will.'

Another dig, and once again she refused to take up the bait. Instead, she made a play of brushing down her plain black dress. The hostility between them was starting to hum again.

Then she heard Dane sigh heavily, and glanced up, her own expression softening into sympathy when she caught him leaning against the doorframe, a long-fingered hand wearily rubbing at his face.

He had hardly been home during the last three days and nights. Where and what he had been doing she didn't know. But each day the strain had shown a little more on him. And by now those usually rock-solid planes of his hard-angled face were scored with tiredness, his eyes sunken into their sockets and bruised.

She grimaced, touching lightly at her own bruised face. It was getting better slowly, the vivid purple clouding to an even uglier muddy green. But the soreness had gone. Her shoulder was not so stiff either now. And physically she was beginning to recover from the accident.

Emotionally was another thing entirely.

Turning away, she opened a small tin on her dressing-table and peeled out a fresh-up pad then walked over to him. 'Here,' she murmured, and reached up to press the cooling pad to his brow. 'This should refresh you a little...'

His eyes flicked open, and arrowed directly on to her own; trembling a little at their closeness, Lily avoided looking into them, her attention fixed on the small white pad and the tight tanned flesh she was pressing it against.

'Why did you marry him, Lily?' he murmured huskily. 'How could you go ahead and marry him when you knew from the very beginning what was happening between me and you?'

Her fingers quivered. 'I loved Daniel, Dane,' she stated quietly. And she did, she insisted silently to herself. In her own way, she did.

'But you wanted me.'

She went to deny it, then stopped, grimacing ruefully to herself. What was the use? He would know she was lying. They couldn't be within three feet of each other without the juices flowing.

'Blonde hair, blue eyes, sweet smile,' he listed huskily when she made no answer, 'face of an angel and the body of a siren. Pity about the mercenary streak in you. Other than that, you're quite perfect, aren't you?'

'Perfect?' She picked up on the word and threw it deridingly back at him. 'Nobody—not even you—is perfect, Dane.'

'I'll never forgive you for deceiving Danny the way you did,' he went on as if she hadn't spoken. 'I'll never forgive you for marrying him despite knowing how I could make you feel! And I'll never, Lily,' he stated thickly, 'forgive you for showing him up to me for the weak-willed pathetic person he was when he allowed you to carry on your affair with Radley right under his very nose!'

'Oh, don't, Dane.' Understanding at last, she placed a gentle hand on his cheek. 'Don't be angry with Daniel. Be angry with me, but not with him. You loved him so!'

'Oh, God,' he choked, and pushed her away from him, a shaking hand going up to rub at his suspiciously moist eyes.

'Dane——' She made a movement to approach him again, but he swung his back to her.

'Five minutes,' he said gruffly. 'We'll expect you in the study in five minutes,' and walked away, leaving Lily trembling with a mixture of pain at his contempt for her and sympathy for a man who was too big a man to weep for the loss of his brother.

She entered the study to find Mr Trent, a tall, thin sallow-faced man, nervously shuffling papers on Daniel's desk. The reason for his nervousness, she noted as she nodded a greeting towards him, was standing tall and forbidding by the study window.

Her heart began to thud. He looked angry and tense, and her glance flicked nervously back to the solicitor, wondering just what had been said before she arrived to put Dane in a temper. But the solicitor's expression was thoroughly impassive, and she realised, on a wave of relief that sent her legs weak, that Mr Trent would not divulge anything to Dane that he had not been given leave to say.

Secrets, she mocked heavily. Too many secrets to make life comfortable.

Moving carefully, she went towards the two spoon-backed chairs placed in front of the desk, sat down in one of them and folded her hands tightly on her lap.

There were a few more minutes of tension-locked silence while she and Mr Trent waited for Dane to join them, then the solicitor's pointed clearing of his throat brought the other man across the room. He sat down stiffly beside Lily.

It was brief and it was simple, mainly because poor Daniel had never really expected this particular will to be read. So in neat, clear forms he had laid out his requirements: some small bequests in recognition of people, old family retainers mostly, who had worked for his grandfather when he had been alive and had loyally stayed on to work for Daniel.

'These people will be informed separately,' Mr Trent explained. 'But the rest, and what amounts to the main bulk of Mr Norfolk's estate, he leaves to his wife Mrs Lily Norfolk.'

'What?' Lily jerked upright in her seat. 'But that isn't right!' she exclaimed, tiny explosions of alarm going off in her head. 'Everything was supposed to go to his brother Dane! I . . .'

'Very convincing,' Dane derided her protest.

'But it's true!' She turned on him, shock holding her blue eyes wide and bright. She couldn't believe this! 'W-we talked about this—just after y-your grandfather's death, and we decided to——' She stopped that sentence, cutting it off before she thoroughly blackened herself in Dane's eyes. 'And D-Daniel decided he should make a will!' she corrected hastily. 'I was to get a lump sum—a lump sum!' she repeated shrilly. 'And the rest was to go to you——'

'Your husband was very specific, Mrs Norfolk.' Sensing a family row beginning to brew, the solicitor cut in firmly. 'There are certain provisos attached to this, of course,' he continued. 'The stud will be yours in effect—only until you re-marry, when it will revert back into Norfolk hands—Mr Dane Norfolk's hands to be precise. Your husband was very concerned that you should feel secure in the event of anything happening to him,' the solicitor murmured reassuringly at her white-faced stare. 'And in the event that you will almost certainly re-marry he has also made certain provisions for you in a lump sum——' he named a figure that made Lily gasp and Dane scoff derisively '—to be held in trust by Mr Dane Norfolk until such time when the stud reverts back into his care. Mr Dane Norfolk will receive immediately any stocks or shares his brother held—the largest and perhaps most important of these being the stock he owned in Norfolk Holdings...'

But Lily wasn't listening; her mind was racing. She couldn't understand it—couldn't work out why Daniel had gone against everything they'd decided upon and left the stud and his money to her! She could feel Dane's eyes on her, hard and cynically accusing, knew what he was thinking and felt the heat run guiltily up her cheeks.

' . . . and a small property Mr Norfolk owned in Chelsea,' Mr Trent continued, 'which he bequeaths to his good friend Mr Mark Radley along with a lump sum of money.'

Oh, God, Lily thought wretchedly. He'd turned everything around! She'd believed she was getting the Chelsea house. Daniel had turned everything around! But why?

'Chelsea?' Like Lily only a moment earlier, Dane jerked upright, his black brows drawing together across his nose. 'What house in Chelsea?' Then, before the solicitor could answer, his head twisted sharply on his shoulders, those silver eyes lancing Lily with a bitter look. 'I don't need to be told, do I, Lily?' he challenged grimly.

'No,' she whispered. 'You already know which one.'

'Radley,' he scowled. 'Bloody Mark Radley is living in it!'

Mr Trent cleared his throat. 'Also to Mr Radley Mr Norfolk leaves certain—personal effects listed in a private letter already in Mrs Norfolk's possession. And other than those few cash payments in recognition of some employees he felt deserved his thanks there is nothing else. As you can tell,' Mr Trent concluded, 'this was not a last will and testament of a man who expected to die so young. It was merely a safeguard against the improbability happening.'

He stood up with a suddenness that said he was aware of the threat of an explosion in the room and wanted to be gone before it happened. He stuffed his papers into a battered old briefcase then came around the desk to offer Lily his hand. She rose and took it, her own fingers icy against his warmer ones. 'Let me offer you my sincere condolences once again, Mrs Norfolk,' he murmured solemnly. 'And if you need me for anything—anything at all, then please feel free to contact me.'

'Yes. I—th-thank you,' Lily stammered, like the solicitor, very aware of Dane's seething anger. It stung into her back, keeping it stiffly erect. 'Th-thank you for everything, Mr Trent.'

With a brief glance at Dane and a mute nod, he turned and left the room, closing the door behind him.

The silence stung. Lily folded her arms across her body and sank back down into the chair. She couldn't believe it. She couldn't believe that Daniel had done this to her. He'd known she never wanted the stud! Just as he'd had to know all this would cause trouble with his brother!

'Well, that's that, then.' Dane stood up, the sombre dark suit he was wearing increasing the air of suppressed anger in him. He walked over to the drinks cabinet and uncapped one of the crystal decanters. 'Only two years of having to play the sweet, simpering angel and you get the jackpot. Not bad, Lily. Not bad at all...'

CHAPTER SIX

'I DIDN'T want any of it,' Lily denied, hugging herself as if cold, the shock of Daniel's will still trembling through her system. 'Not the stud, his money—none of it.'

' "The lady doth protest too much, methinks",' Dane drawled provokingly.

'It's the truth,' she declared. 'And Daniel knew it.' Which made it all the more puzzling as to why he had done this to her. He's tied me down! she realised on an angry start. He's tied me down to this damned place when he knew I've been straining at the leash to get away! 'If you must know the truth,' she snapped out irritably as she stood up, 'I hate this place!'

'The truth, Lily?' Dane mocked cynically. 'Since when have you ever dealt in the truth?'

As of now, she thought angrily. 'If there was any way I could alter what he's done, I would do.'

'There is,' Dane said, watching her through narrowed eyes as she moved restlessly around the room. Her agitation intrigued him. He wasn't at all sure what was causing it. 'Marry Radley. Then the whole lot will revert to me.'

'What?' she spun around to stare at him, her expression quite comical to him simply because he was reading it all wrong. 'Marry Mark?' she choked out incredulously.

'He's been your damned lover for long enough.' He shrugged. 'Why not make it all nice and proper now that Daniel's gone?'

'How many times do I have to tell you that Mark is not my lover?' she cried, closing her eyes in an effort to hang on to some semblance of self-control.

'As many times as you like, but I won't believe you,' Dane replied. 'What did you do, hmm? Did you wait for Danny to go to sleep at night then creep out of his bed into Radley's?'

'That's a terrible thing to say!' she gasped.

'No more terrible than you having your lover sleeping next door!'

'I refuse to listen to any of this.' On legs that were far from steady she turned to the door.

But Dane was quick. He came across the gap separating them like lightning, his hand curling painfully around her arm to spin her around to face him. 'Oh, no, you don't,' he murmured threateningly. 'You don't leave here until you give me a reasonable explanation as to why Radley had the connecting bedroom to yours!'

'He didn't!' she denied. 'He slept in his studio when he stayed here!' A custom-made room on the second floor of the house.

'But you forget,' Dane persisted. 'And one should always have a good memory when they lie as much as you do, Lily. But I caught Radley red-handed in that very room only the other day.' She started jerkily, and his mouth compressed into a satisfied smile. 'Your housekeeper had left your case in your room for me to collect. I walked into what I assumed was your room—yours and Daniel's room!' he punctuated harshly. 'And found Radley sitting at the bureau in there, sorting out his things!'

Lily dampened her dry lips, her heart beginning to pound sluggishly in her chest. This was very shaky ground. 'Daniel's things,' she corrected huskily. 'It—it was D-Daniel's room. Mark was going through Daniel's things.'

'Daniel's——? What bloody right did he have to go through my brother's things?'

'Y-you heard Daniel's will,' she said nervously. 'He had left certain—personal things to Mark. M-Mark already knew what they were and had come to collect them.'

'With whose permission?'

'I . . .' God, Lily closed her eyes. With no one's permission, she admitted silently. He had done it out of concern for her. He had done it because he'd already decided he was not coming to Daniel's funeral, that that visit here was going to be his last.

But—God, how was she supposed to explain all of that to Dane without having to answer more questions, field more bitter accusations?

Her legs went to jelly suddenly, the energy required to maintain this level of self-defence draining the life out of her, and she swayed dizzily within the hard clutch of his fingers. 'M-may I sit down, please?' she murmured, lifting a trembling hand to her head. 'I suddenly feel a little——'

'God damn and blast it!' Dane muttered, catching her to him as she wilted into a faint. 'God damn and blast you, Lily!'

Grimly, he gathered her into his arms and walked out of the study, his expression harsh as he carried her up the stairs and laid her on her own bed.

Her own bed. Something ripped inside him, sending him swinging around to glare at the closed door which connected this room with the one next door. Daniel's room, she'd called it. Daniel's. He strode over to it and threw it open, then stood, slashing his gaze over the old, familiar contents inside. He walked over to the wardrobe and opened the doors. Daniel's clothes. He would recognise them anywhere. Daniel's books on the shelves. Moving to the bed, he snatched up one of several framed photographs sitting on the bedside table. It was Lily, adorned in her wedding gown of white lace. Laughing up at Daniel. He picked another frame. Himself—his eyes went hot. Himself astride one of Grandfather's huge stallions, looking cool and arrogant, superbly in control of the big beast.

'That's it, big brother!' the tease echoed down through the years. 'Show us your worth.' Click— the camera had captured the scene forever.

That was just before Lily had come on the scene. Before he had stopped coming here as a regular visitor. Before he'd found he had it in him to lust after his brother's wife!

He put the frame down, teeth clenched tightly to ward off the well of emotion building inside him. Another frame stood beside the other two. He picked that up, then felt all the burning anger inside him congeal into one vicious ball of violence. It was Lily—Lily smiling up at the man who had his arms around her. Radley, smiling down at her. On an act of violence that left him shaking afterwards, he turned and hurled the frame across the room, watching starkly as it hit the opposite wall and crashed to the floor, the glass breaking, splintering into a hundred tiny pieces.

Why the hell should Danny want to keep a photograph like that by his bed? Was he blind? Totally blind to what was going on around him? Why had he and Lily slept in separate rooms?

Determined to get some answers, no matter how sick it made Lily feel to have them dragged out of her, he swung back into the other bedroom——

Then stopped, halted by the sight of her lying there looking so small and defenceless. The black mourning dress she was wearing did nothing for her except accentuate the fine quality of her skin. His loins kicked him, and he spun away bitterly, despising himself for being able to respond so basically at a time like this.

He went to stand by the window, thrusting his hands into his pockets as he stared out bleakly, waiting for her to come round.

Life goes on, he acknowledged heavily as he watched a string of horses gallop across the high pasture to the left of the house. The owner had been buried only this morning, but his charges still needed their exercise.

Lily's charges now, he realised. Lily's responsibility.

A soft sound behind him had him swinging back to face the room. Lily was rubbing her brow, long, incredibly slender fingers mesmerising him as they stroked lightly across her smooth skin.

She saw him standing across the room and went still for a moment, remembering. Then she struggled up and swung her feet to the floor. 'I need a drink of water,' she said, trying to get up, but the room swayed dizzily and she had to close her eyes again.

'Wait there,' he clipped. 'I'll get it.' Dane walked into her bathroom and, gladly, Lily let her dizzy head fall back on to the pillows. 'Here.'

Sitting himself down beside her, he reached out to slide a hand beneath her nape, helping her rise enough to sip at the cool glass of water. But when she'd indicated that she'd had enough he didn't move away but remained sitting there, the glass discarded on to her bedside table, before he leaned forwards to place his elbows on his spread knees.

She studied him in silence for a while, seeing the tension and the emotional tiredness in his grim, taut profile. His hips were resting against her legs, warm and oddly comforting when really they should threaten—threaten to light all those forbidden feelings she harboured for Dane. He had removed his jacket at some point, and his white shirt clung to the muscles in his long back. His hair, straight and black and expertly cut, was, as always, immaculate, even though she had seen him scrape impatient fingers through it on countless occasions today.

He looked at her suddenly, surprising her with the quick twist of his head so that their eyes clashed—and held, trapping the breath inside her lungs because she knew that, just as his eyes were revealing his feelings, so were her own.

He wanted her. She wanted him. Would it ever be otherwise while they both persisted in denying it? Perhaps she should just give in, let him take her. It would only take a small gesture for him to know what she was asking for, and he would accept. That much she was in no doubt of. Not while the delicate vibration of her senses pulsed warmly like this, given life by the expression in his darkened eyes.

And in the taking would the need go away?

She didn't think so. Oh, maybe for him it would, she accepted bleakly. Dane was a very sensual man. You only had to count the long list of women who had passed through his life to know that. But for herself?

'Just answer me one thing,' he demanded gruffly. 'Why did you and Daniel have separate rooms?'

Miserably, she closed her eyes, shutting him out. What was not to be was not to be, she told herself grimly. It had been too easy for him to dismiss the sensations passing between them.

'You said yourself once,' she answered flatly, 'that Daniel was not very—physical.'

'So it was through necessity that you took Radley as your lover?'

Where it came from she had no idea unless it was the result of those few moments of honesty they had just shared with their eyes, but fury surged like fire through her, forcing her upright on the bed. 'I am sick of being forced to justify myself to you!' she cried. 'It's none of your business, damn you! None of your business!'

'It's my business that you've been playing my brother for a fool!' he grated, grasping hold of her as she went to fling herself off the bed. He gave her a shake. 'The two of you,' he went on harshly. 'You and Radley, gazing lovingly at each other over your coffee-cups even before you married Daniel!' He shook her again, his fingers biting hard into her upper arms. 'The two of you gazing at each other in a photograph my brother keeps on his bedside table! What does that make Danny but a bloody blind fool?'

'Oh, God.' Lily sucked in a shaky breath. 'Daniel was no one's fool, Dane,' she whispered tiredly. 'And you're the one who was bloody blind!'

'Me?' he choked incredulously. 'How can I be the blind one when I saw through your disguise almost from the start?'

'You saw what you wanted to see,' she corrected.

'Which is what?' he challenged.

No. Lily shut her eyes and mouth tightly. She would not let herself say it. She would not!

'Come on, Lily,' he challenged gratingly. 'You've just made a very provoking statement there and I want you to explain it. Explain it, damn you!' he exploded when she continued to sit there with her mind shut tight on him.

'Let me go,' she breathed.

'The hell I'll let you go,' he refused, tightening his grip on her. 'And I never will do until I get the damned truth out of you!'

'Which truth?' Her eyes flicked open, bright with pain and an anger that announced the end of her control. 'Your truth or the real truth? Your truth says I lie, I cheat, I sleep around with any man who will have me! Is that what you want to hear, Dane? Is it? Is it?'

'Yes,' he hissed. 'That's exactly what I want to hear!' With a lurch, he threw his body across hers, his hands grasping her face, holding it imprisoned while his gaze burned into her. 'Anyone, Lily? You'll have anyone? Then I think it's my turn— long past my bloody turn!'

'No——!'

His dark head swooped, cutting off her shrill protest, demanding, with a ruthlessness that set her reeling, a hungry response from her. But she refused to give it, battled not to give it, squirming, hitting out at him with her feet and fists, tossing her head from side to side in an effort to avoid him.

She was wrong, was her last coherent thought as Dane quickly and cruelly contained every attempt she made to escape him. The sexual tension had not eased, it was ricocheting off every sense they possessed, boiling them up into this hot, seething mass of sexual fury.

Forcing her lips apart and gaining entry to her mouth was the catalyst, the new heated intimacy tumbling like an explosion through her. She groaned, then stretched sensuously, sending her seeking body arching against his. And he let out a grunt of triumph.

'Easy, Lily, easy,' he jeered as she went like liquid beneath him.

Yes, she acknowledged wretchedly. She was easy for him.

Their legs stopped fighting and tangled sensuously instead, his long, taut-muscled and strong, hers shorter, smoother and much, much more sensitive to the tensile power in his. The thin cloth of her black dress was no barrier, and as he pressed himself against her she felt the hard evidence of his desire surge against her thighs with a quivering uplift of her own sensual pleasure.

She gasped his name, her arms wrapping around him, restless, desperate to feel his flesh beneath her fingers. But his shirt was in the way. She tugged at it fretfully, opening her mouth to deepen the kiss at the same time, not wanting to lose contact with him, terrified to in case reality stepped in and hit them both with a cold, hard sense of what they were doing.

Dane grunted, reaching between them to grasp hold of his shirt, and proceeded to wrench the buttons apart. He lifted her, his hand flat on her back, mouth urgently tasting her arching throat as he slid down the back zip of her dress. It became a dark puddle of sombre black on the floor beside the bed. Her bra followed, and Lily wound herself around him, straining to get closer, needing him, crazed with it.

The whole thing was crazy, a madness attacking them both out of nowhere, wild and mindless.

He kissed her until her lips throbbed, then transferred his hunger to her breasts, licking, suckling, coaxing, urging broken little gasps of pleasure from her while her fingers stroked the slick, smooth skin of his back, nails scoring it, palms kneading.

Dane muttered something that was both a vicious curse aimed directly at her and a vile acknowledgement of his own complete loss of control. And he took her mouth again, smothering it as he grasped one of her restless hands and dragged it down his body until he'd placed it where he wanted it most to be. She gasped, shocked to her very roots by the sweet, pulsing intimacy. But before she could even think of pulling away his own hand had slid along her thighs and she became lost in more sensation—the kind that made her cry out his name, arch, then go tensely still as tiny coloured explosions began hurling themselves at the backs of her eyes.

The sound of a tentative knocking at the bedroom door had them both clattering back down to earth with a resounding bump. 'God!' Dane choked, landing on his feet with no idea of how he came to be there. His torso was heaving, the thick matt of dark, curling hair on his chest spiked with sweat. His eyes were glazed and glittering fiercely, cheeks wearing the dark hue of desire, his hair muzzed.

Hair muzzed. Shuddering at what the sight of him did to her, Lily closed her eyes and turned over, curling herself into a tight ball of shame.

The knock came again. Dane bent over and flicked the edge of the duvet over her. It was only then that she realised she was lying here almost naked. Naked and wanton and ashamed of herself.

'I despise you, Lily,' he said harshly. 'I despise you for the way you've used my brother—and for the way you coolly and cold-bloodedly fleeced him of everything he had—even his bloody pride, by the way things look here.' His eyes slashed around the room. 'But most of all I despise you for the way you let me touch you like that only hours after you've buried him.'

'Get out,' she whispered. That was all—what else could she say? She was well aware of just how bad things looked for her. But as she listened to his angry tread making for the door the tears began to fall, hot and heavy. And for once she was crying for herself alone.

Alone. Alone with the lies. Alone with the mess Daniel's death had left her with.

When, eventually, she found the courage to go back downstairs to face him again, it was to find Dane had gone. Back to London, she was told. No, he had left no message.

Which just about finished it, she concluded bleakly.

A sudden dire need to feel clean, fresh air on her face had her collecting a lightweight jacket and walking quickly out of the house. She walked, just walked for hours thinking. By the time tiredness and the growing darkness drew her back to the house, she had come to some firm decisions.

Refusing Mrs Jakes's concerned offer of a light dinner, she took herself straight off to bed, and slept deeply right through the long night. The next morning she awoke with those same decisions she'd come to the afternoon before still firm in her mind, and set about putting them into practice.

She began by calling Australia, and her parents. They were happy to hear from her, and even happier when she informed them of her intentions. After that, she took herself off to the stables, going in search of Jack Mason, Daniel's stable manager, and found him in the small office situated at the end of the main stable block. A small, thick-set man who had worked alongside Daniel's grandfather for years before giving Daniel the same kind of support, he glanced up from the stack of paperwork he was studying as she entered, and grimaced to himself, almost as if he'd been expecting her to call on him like this.

'I need your help, Jack,' Lily said once the expected formalities were done with. 'I've decided to go away for a while, but first I have to know that this place will be in safe hands while I'm gone.'

That was all it took. Just those few simple words and the wary expression left his face to be replaced with a look she was far more used to seeing on his affable face. It only occurred to her then that maybe he was worried about the safety of his own job.

'Tell me what you want,' he said, 'and I'll promise to see to it.'

Half an hour later, she walked back to the house feeling as if at least one of the burdens Daniel had left her with had been lifted from her shoulders.

It took a couple of weeks, but by then she had transferred all her own responsibilities towards the stud over to Jack. He had been able to recommend one of the younger men working for him who he felt was ready to take on more responsibility, and between them they split the extra duties of Lily's own clerical role in the running of things, and, more importantly, the gap left by Daniel's death between the two of them.

After that, it was just a case of making travel arrangements, packing up, leaving Mrs Jakes in charge of the house and driving away. She was going to Australia, and as far away from the stud, and the Norfolk name, as she could get.

The stud meant nothing to her any more. Nothing.

Her flight was due to take off early in the morning, so she chose to spend her last night in England at a hotel close to the airport to make the transfer from it to the plane more simple.

Simple. She knew from the moment the telephone began ringing in the room she had been given for the night that nothing could ever be that simple. Premonition, sense of dread, call it what you liked, she wasn't surprised to hear Dane's voice come rasping down the line when she lifted the receiver to her ear.

'I want to see you,' he gritted.

'No,' she refused. 'I—I don't want to see you.'

'I'm not really giving you any choice in the matter, Lily,' he informed her uncompromisingly. 'I'm in the hotel lobby. I'm coming up.'

Snap—the line went dead, and with it went the almost serene sense of peace she had managed to shroud herself in since her last disastrous meeting with Dane.

Her legs went weak, sending her sinking shakily on to the bed, her heart thumping sluggishly in her breast, tension already beginning to lock the slender stretch of her shoulders. And all before she'd so much as laid eyes on him.

The knock at her door brought her jerking to her feet, her sluggish heart suddenly taking on a hectic pound.

What did he want? She stood there staring at the locked door, wondering if she dared just ignore him, refuse to let him in. What else was there left for him to do to her? Couldn't he have just let her bow out gracefully? Did he have to keep on tormenting her like——?

Another knock, harder this time. Her fingers shook as she raked them agitatedly through her short, silky hair. Then she was drawing them down the sides of her short blue Lycra dress and walking slowly towards the door, drawn there by a will much stronger than her own.

He was dressed more casually than she was used to seeing him, in a wine-coloured short-sleeved silk shirt, tucked loosely into the waistband of his fashionably pleated cream trousers. But his hair, as always, was short, sleek and so superbly styled that her fingers itched to reach up and muzz it the way they had when they——

'What the hell are you playing at now, Lily?' he demanded, pushing by her as if he had a right to just barge in and out of her life.

She blinked, having no idea what he was getting at. Closing the door, she turned to watch him begin prowling the room restlessly, his body stiff with angry tension as he picked things up, put them down again, opened the door to her bathroom, closed it again, swung over to her suitcases stacked neatly against a wall, flicked at the flight tags dangling from them, then straightened again, not once glancing in her direction.

What exactly was he looking for? she wondered. What did he hope to——?

A sudden thought brought a red-hot tide of anger washing up her face. 'I'm not meeting Mark here for a dirty weekend, if that's what you're thinking!' she said stiffly. 'In case it has escaped your notice, I don't need to sink to those depths any more.'

Stopping his prowling, at last he turned to face her, running brooding, heavily hooded eyes over her. 'It would be damned difficult for you both,' he muttered, 'with you still here in London and him in Hong Kong.'

Hong Kong? She stared at him. 'What's he doing there?' The last she'd heard, Mark was in southern France, drowning his sorrows on a Riviera beach.

'Quit the blank look, Lily,' he derided. 'You know exactly what Radley is doing there—basically the same as he did here, and painting his wretched soul into the expensive racehorses the wealthy Chinese covet over there with such a passion, while waiting for you to join him.'

CHAPTER SEVEN

WAS he? It was the first she'd heard of it. Mark had been in touch with her only once since Daniel's death, and that was just to get her to send some of his things out to him in France.

She glanced curiously at Dane. 'How do you know where Mark is?' she asked. 'And more to the point—why should it interest you at all?'

'It interests me for many reasons,' he clipped. 'And I know because I made it my business to know.'

'The same as you've made it your business to check up on my movements?' she asked indignantly, then sighed impatiently. 'Look,' she said. It hurt to look at him. It hurt to be in the same room as him! She didn't know why he had bothered coming here if all he wanted to do was throw more accusations at her. And she wanted him gone—just as quickly as she could get him through the door. 'I'm not getting into another slanging match with you, Dane. So if that's all you've come here for, then I would appreciate it if you would just leave. I have an early flight in the morning, and . . .'

'To Australia,' he nodded, making no move to take the hint and go. 'Making the stop-over in Hong Kong by any chance?'

'For what purpose?' she snapped. 'So Mark and I can gloat over our Norfolk coup?' It was meant as a joke—albeit an acid one, but as usual Dane was more than willing to believe the worst of her, bitter contempt flashing at her from those silver-ice eyes of his.

'Couldn't you wait longer than a month before going to him?' he demanded gratingly. 'Would it have been such a hardship to pretend grief for my brother's death for just a few months longer?'

'What's it to you what I do?' she snapped irritably, coming away from the door and walking over to the window so that she didn't have to look at him.

'I'm warning you now, Lily,' he said tightly. 'Before you do something you may later regret. I don't want you bringing Radley back with you to live at the stud.'

'What I do and don't do at the stud or anywhere else is none of your damned business!' How many times had she repeated that over the last few weeks? How many times had Dane taken it upon himself to poke his nose into her affairs?

'Remember Daniel's will,' he grated warningly. 'The moment you marry Radley, the stud and all you've worked for reverts to me!'

So, he'd got her marrying Mark now! 'What a good idea!' she drawled, turning to send him a hard, false smile. 'Perhaps if I do find myself a new husband it will get you and your filthy insinuations off my damned back!'

'Marry Radley at your damned peril!'

'Then go home with an easy mind, Dane.' Some bitter little devil inside her made her say what he expected to hear. 'Because I have no intention of putting at risk anything Daniel left me by marrying anyone!'

He took the bait, his eyes flaring with contempt. 'Mercenary bitch!' he ground out. 'I always knew you were a mercenary bitch!'

'That's right,' she agreed, 'Lily the whoring opportunist!' On a sigh she spun around to face him, eyes alight with bitterness. They'd had this scene before. 'I'll live up to all your suspicions about me, Dane,' she promised him acidly, 'and sleep my way through a million men without jeopardising my wonderful inheritance by marrying any of them!'

'Starting with Radley in Hong Kong, no doubt!'

God, she'd had enough of this! 'I'm going to Australia to be with my family, Dane! Not Hong Kong. Nowhere near Hong Kong!'

And pigs might fly, his deriding expression said.

On a burst of angry energy, she walked over to her suitcases, grabbed up her fight bag and unzipped it. 'Singapore!' she snapped, thrusting her flight tickets at him. 'My stop-over is in Singapore, damn you. Not Hong Kong!'

He checked them. He couldn't just take her word for it, he had to check the damned tickets before he could believe her. On a sound of disgust she moved away from him, back to the window where she could aim all the hurt she was feeling at the steadily darkening evening sky outside.

'All right,' he muttered after a moment. 'I jumped to conclusions.'

'The wrong conclusions.'

He shifted uncomfortably. 'I apologise.'

Hardly mollified by his reluctant apology, she glared at him, her breasts still heaving on the pressure of anger still bubbling inside her. 'How did you find out I was going away?'

He shrugged. 'Mrs Jakes told me. I—I rang you at the stud. I—needed to see you.'

See me? 'What for?' The way she'd read it, they'd said it all the last time they were together.

Her bewildered look brought a short laugh huffing from him. 'You know what for, Lily,' he bit out. And it was his turn to spin away, his shoulders hunching inside the maroon silk shirt. 'It isn't getting any easier. In fact, it's getting bloody worse.'

Was it? She stared at him in silence for a while, then sighed heavily because she knew he was right. It was getting worse. With no Daniel to act as a buffer against all this sexual tension, they just seemed to explode on sight.

'Then maybe it's a good thing I'm going away,' she said.

If she expected him to deny it, she was in for a disappointment. Dane just nodded in grim agreement. 'How long do you intend to be away?' he enquired instead.

'Six months—a year maybe,' she shrugged, hoping he didn't hear the telling little catch in her voice. 'I n-need the break.'

Again he nodded in total agreement. 'And the stud?' he enquired.

Lily's smile was wry. Was that really what this visit was all about, the precious Norfolk stud? 'Oh, don't worry,' she assured him drily. 'I've made sure it won't suffer from my defection.' She went on to tell him what she'd arranged. 'Jack's own good reputation should ease the minds of any clients who are concerned by Daniel's death. My own involvement was purely clerical and therefore not that important.'

'The place was never run on the reliance of its paying clients,' Dane also pointed out. 'Its reputation relies on the quality of its private stock.'

Which seemed to say it all.

Needing something to do other than just stand there tormenting herself by drinking in his presence, Lily picked up her tickets where Dane had placed them on the table and went to put them away again.

He watched her every move, making her fumble self-consciously with the zip on her flight bag. Inevitably, it stuck, and her fingers were trembling by the time she managed to free it then close it.

'Just tell me one thing,' he burst out suddenly. 'If it was a straight choice now, between me and Radley, who would you choose?'

The pressure in her chest stopped her breathing as she slowly straightened up, her mind refusing to believe what she had just heard him say.

'I—I d-don't understand,' she whispered unsteadily.

'Yes, you do.' Suddenly he was standing right behind her, his breath warm on her nape. 'I'm asking you to tell me whether Radley means more to you than I do.'

Her heart began to quiver, her throat drying up on a hope she had never dared allow herself before—a hope she didn't dare allow herself now, she told herself, not trusting that roughened tone in his voice. He could just be playing with her, wanting to see if he could at last bring her to her knees for him.

'I—I don't know,' she whispered in the end. 'It isn't that——' Simple, she had been going to say. But he cut in, his voice roughening even more.

'Then make it six months,' he said. 'Six months has to be long enough for you to get all the comfort you need from your parents, grieve for my brother, and decide what it is you want to do with the rest of your life. And whether it's Radley you want or whether it's me. Only you can make that decision, Lily; neither I nor Radley can make it for you. But if you decide it is me you want, then you contact me.' He sucked in a deep, tension-locked breath and let it out again. 'But you give yourself those six months before you make a move on either of us—understand?'

No, she didn't understand. Was too frightened to even dare to understand! Putting his insinuations about Mark to one side, what was he hinting at for them? Sex—affairs? Love—permanency?

Jerking around to face him, she searched his silver-grey eyes. 'And what about you?' she wanted to know. 'What will you be doing during these six very specific months?'

'The same as you, I expect,' he shrugged. 'Living my life, going about my business as I have always done. Why?' he then drawled deridingly. 'What do you want me to do—stay at home, wear my heart on my sleeve for you?'

'You don't possess a heart,' she derided his derision, stung by it. 'You possess a damned healthy sex-drive, and that's about all!'

He muttered something and caught hold of her. 'If it is just sex, then we're both suffering from the same problem!' he rasped. 'Just as we both know this has no chance of working for us right now! It's right that we put some distance between us! Right we try to make this—thing at least appear decent!'

Thing? He called her love for him a *thing*? But he was right, she had to acknowledge. Whatever it was between them had no chance of becoming anything more than a sordid little interlude until decency had been upheld.

She was his brother's widow after all.

'And—if I decide after six months that it's you I want, what if you've changed your mind about me?'

'It's a two-way risk, Lily,' he pointed out. 'And neither of us can predict the outcome, can we?'

Then she didn't want to go! He was actually giving her real reason to hope at last, and she wanted to stay right here and shorten the risks! She wanted to throw herself into his arms and beg him to love her—love her until he couldn't love her any more! And damn the decency in it! 'I want you now,' she choked, and on a small sob moved in closer to him, winding her arms around his body and pressing her face into his chest.

'Oh, Lily...' He sighed. His hands coming around her made her shudder with pleasure, and she pressed herself closer. 'Six months isn't so long. And, let's face it,' he added heavily, 'it should be twelve. But even I'm not prepared to lengthen the stakes that much. And it's my business to risk long shots every day of my life.'

He was trying to make light of it, but his eyes as he gently turned her face up to his were dark and driven. And when her lips parted and quivered on a broken sob he muttered something not very nice, and crushed his mouth down on to her own.

It was back to where they had left off the last time. As soon as their mouths touched, she was flung back into that wild restless vortex Dane had hurled her into weeks ago on her bed at the stud.

The instant, hot curl of excitement unfurled inside her and blasted out to every corner of her body, her hands curling into the tight, hot skin at his waist, clinging for dear life, her body trembling with a need that brought a groan of anguish wrenching from him.

'I was determined not to do this,' he muttered. But his mouth was hot and hungry, offering no hint of withdrawing. The eager parting of her lips and the greedy invasion of his tongue sent her whirling over the edge on a rush of pure sensation that ripped right through her. She heard him gasp and knew he'd felt the same thing too.

They seemed to fuse then, their mouths twisting, their tongues coiling, her breasts hardening into twin peaks that fused themselves against the hectic heave of his chest—and his hips, pulsing against her own, threatening to hurl the whole thing way out of control.

'Stay,' she whispered. 'Just for tonight. Stay with me?' She didn't even care any more that she was literally begging him to make love to her.

'God in heaven,' he groaned. But his arms locked around her arching body so that he could lift her off the ground, and she helped by moving with him, holding hungrily on to his mouth as he carried her over to the waiting bed.

One night, she told herself weakly as they fell in a tangle of limbs on to the soft duvet. Would it matter that much if they stole just one short night? She needed this—it—him. Had done for so long now that she suddenly knew she would die of starvation if he went away now.

It was like being caught by a wild fever, Dane kissing, caressing her with a need that hinted strangely at desperation. But he gentled slowly, turning the kiss away from hunger into a deep, drugging sensuality that she wanted to go on forever. Their clothes fell away by degrees, his shirt, her dress, his trousers, her scrappy underwear, until they were lying on their sides, bodies melded down the front. And with that subtle expertise he was so famous for he began to build up that intolerable pressure inside her, building and building, until she was thoroughly supple in his arms, breathless, gasping for his mercy. It was then and only then that he at last rolled on top of her and surely slid his body into hers——

Then stopped, his head coming up to stare at her in utter disbelief. 'Lily?' he choked.

'No.' Jerkily she covered his mouth with her hand. 'No, it doesn't matter.'

Dane stayed tense and still, the shock of his discovery putting a stunned grey cast to his face.

Terrified that he was going to withdraw from her, Lily moved, sending him forging through the silken barrier with a soft cry that was both pain and pleasure. He swallowed thickly, shook his head, then, as her unused body closed tightly around him, he groaned, and gave in, closing his lids over the bewildered glaze in his eyes as he began to move——

Slowly at first, until the deep, sensual rhythm enveloped them both, then he increased it, hardened it, his teeth clenching and the air hissing out from his lungs as though anger had joined in with the passion, and instead of coaxing her into climax with him he impelled her there, leaving her stunned and wasted as she floated slowly back down to earth.

Dane slid away from her, burying his face in the pillow while he fought to gather his scattered senses. Then slowly he turned his head to one side, looking at her, watching her as she lay beside him, eyes closed, her face pale, wearing a look of exhausted awe.

His body stirred, a response to the masculine pride it filled him with to know that he had put that expression on her face.

Him and no other man.

Then what did that make his brother? God in heaven! He jerked away from her as though she stung, his eyes narrowed and bitter on her lovely lying face.

'Why?' he bit out the moment he saw the stirring of life seep back into her body.

She opened languid, beautifully sated eyes to find him looming over her, his dark face tight.

'I'm—sorry,' she whispered, biting down on her bottom lip, at a loss how else to answer him.

'Sorry?' he choked out hoarsely, flaming fury leaping out from his eyes. 'Sorry for what?' he exploded. 'Sorry for cheating my brother out of what you just gave me? Or sorry you gave in to me at all?'

'Sorry I couldn't help myself,' she sighed, coming back down to earth with a resounding bump. Back to fighting, she noted grimly. Back to accusations, suspicions, and, of course, the neverending round of lies. 'Excuse me.' She tried to push him aside. 'I want to get up——'

'You're going nowhere until you've given me some answers!' he snarled, pinning back down on the bed. 'So start talking—now!'

Giving up on the lopsided struggle, she settled back against the pillows. 'Why did I let you make love to me?' She stared up at him, cool challenge in her blue eyes. 'God, I don't know,' she sighed. 'Perhaps because I thought it was what you wanted too.'

His mouth tightened at her mocking tone. 'Why did Daniel never make love to you?' he demanded to know.

'Why? For goodness' sake, Dane!' she muttered impatiently. 'How many clues do you have to have before you work the whole thing out for yourself?'

'Daniel loved you. That much I'm bloody sure of!'

'Did he?' Her tone was sceptical to say the least. 'He loved the stud. And that is the only thing I'm bloody sure about.'

'What's that supposed to mean?'

'At the risk of repeating myself, work it out for yourself. Now I want to get up. Will you please——?'

She got no further. On an angry growl, Dane pinned her to the bed, throwing himself on top of her so that the air was pushed forcefully out of her lungs. 'That wasn't very nice of you,' she gasped.

'Didn't you know? I'm not a very nice person.'

She nodded. 'The complete antithesis of your brother,' she agreed.

'Another cryptic dig?' he drawled. 'I never was any good at cryptic puzzles, Lily. So why don't you give me the answers?'

'They're not mine to give,' she refused.

'Then whose are they?'

'Daniel's.'

'He's dead.'

She nodded, lips tight. 'Too late, then, for your precious answers.'

'You bitch!'

'Oh, we're back to the insults as well, are we?' On another burst of anger, Lily threw herself sideways, managing to free the top half of her body from beneath his. 'You seduce then insult,' she snapped out deridingly as she struggled to free the rest of herself from beneath him. 'If I'm a bitch— what does that make you? Let me go!' she spat when he grabbed at her flailing arms.

'Not until I get the full truth out of you,' he refused, yanking her back towards him.

'The truth?' She landed in a seething mass of naked flesh against him. 'You're always searching for the truth!'

Her eyes glinted up at him with tears of hurt and bitter frustration. His didn't shift from their grim, determined glare.

'All right, Dane,' she surrendered tiredly. 'Which truth would you like this time—the one you prefer to hear or the one I know for a bloody fact you will not want to hear?'

'The real truth!' he bit out impatiently. 'The only actual truth there is!'

'Oh, no.' Lily shook her angry head. 'Nothing ever comes in straight black and white. I thought you would have accepted that after the—farce we've just performed here in this bed! The truth has different shades of grey in between—one to suit everyone's needs—including yours!'

'Stop playing games,' he growled, and subdued her easily when she began fighting him again. 'It seems to me, Lily, that you've spent most of your life playing games with other people's feelings! Well, not with me—not any more!'

Is that what he really thought? 'OK...' Her over-bright eyes revealed a sudden hardness that surprised even Dane. 'Then you shall have it—the full, shocking, bloody distasteful lot of it. And let's just see how good it makes you feel! Daniel was never my lover because he was Mark's lover,' she told him. 'Have you got that, Dane? Daniel and Mark were——'

His hands made contact with her shoulders with just enough force to render her silent.

'Liar!' he barked. 'That's just another of your filthy lies! Daniel was not that way! Say it, Lily!' he insisted hoarsely. 'Say it, damn you. Tell me that what you've just said was a lie!'

Her eyes fixed in bitter sympathy on his blanched white face. 'All right,' she murmured quietly. 'It was a lie.'

But it wasn't. And Dane knew it. Somehow he knew that this time she was telling him the truth. And for a moment he just lay there, staring down at her with a kind of hell in his eyes. Then, on a muffled choke, he was lurching off the bed, bending to snatch up his clothes, dragging them on, his movements stiff and jerky, fingers fumbling, hair muzzed.

Oh, God. She closed her eyes against the wave of heated knowledge that rippled through her body.

This was Dane, the man she loved. The man she had just given herself to with all the naked passion she had in her—the man she had just alienated with the truth. The damned, blasted bloody truth.

Feeling sick, Lily climbed off the bed and picked up her short satin robe, tying it securely around her waist. The silence between them was stunning. Dane had moved to sit on a chair, his dark head bent over while he pulled on his socks and shoes, hiding the grim white cast of his face from view. And between them lay the rumpled bed, disparaging her for what had just happened on it.

The sickness swelled on a surge of aching wretchedness, and she lifted pleading eyes to him, her voice thick with distress.

'I'm sorry,' she whispered. 'I never wanted to tell you—was determined not to, but...' Her eyes drifted to the bed again and wretched tears began to burn at her eyes. 'Please!' she pleaded to him. 'Let me——' Explain, she was going to say. But he cut her off.

'No!' he burst out, coming jerkily to his feet. 'Don't say another word! Not another bloody word.'

Not even bothering to look at her again, he turned towards the door.

He's going to walk out on me, Lily realised painfully. He's just going to——

On a sudden upsurge of panic, she threw herself at the door, flattening her body against it, blocking his exit. She was trembling, her face white, breasts heaving beneath the thin covering of her cream satin robe.

'Get out of my way, Lily,' he said flatly.

She shook her head. 'Y-you're not leaving,' she stammered. 'Not without l-letting me explain. N-not without at least trying to understand.'

Grim mouth tightening, he reached for the doorhandle, but Lily covered it with her hand. His own snapped back so quickly that it was clear he didn't want to touch her—actually physically balked at the mere idea of it. And that hurt, hurt so much that a gasp of pain wrenched at her throat.

'You owe me that much!' she cried. 'For all the rotten insults you've thrown at me! But most of all because of what we just shared—right there in that bed!' She glared at the bed, still rumpled from their passionate coupling, and felt sick inside. 'Y-you owe me the chance to explain, Dane...' she whispered thickly.

He said nothing, his mouth drawn tight, eyes so hard and cold that she shivered visibly. But at least he made no further move to leave. Instead he shoved his hands into his pockets and turned away, going over to the small fridge and getting himself a brandy, pouring it into a glass then drinking it down without facing her again.

White and shaking, Lily wilted against the door, uncertain now that she had managed to stop him going just what she was going to say to him. All she did know was that things had gone too far this time to just let him walk away from it all.

It couldn't go on—*she* couldn't go on feeling like this. Tomorrow she was leaving the country, but before she went Dane was going to hear the lot of it. She was sick of the lies, sick of him always believing the worst of her, no matter how much she gave of herself in the hopes of proving otherwise.

'Well?' Dane turned to face her again, the hard clip of his voice shrivelling her inside as much as the cold look in his eyes. 'You seem to think I owe you a hearing—so talk.'

Lily swallowed thickly. 'Daniel wasn't my friend, he was Mark's,' she began. 'M-Mark and I have known each other since we were children. We went to the same schools, moved in the same crowd, everything. When we applied for college places, we thought it great that we happened to be going to the same university, even though we were taking different subjects.'

'Childhood sweethearts?' he jeered.

'No! Childhood friends!' she corrected. 'I've always known what Mark was from the first moment I knew what sex was all about, but I didn't know about Daniel until Sonia Cranston came on the scene.'

'Sonia Cranston?' Dane picked up on the name instantly. 'What does she have to do with any of this?'

'Everything.' Lily pushed her hair off her forehead with a shaky hand. 'She was blackmailing Daniel.'

Sonia. Tall, leggy, fresh-faced Sonia. She was crazy about horses and even crazier about Daniel. 'She chased after him all through the summer recess at the stud, then began travelling up to Oxford to continue her pursuit there.'

'Because Daniel had a thing going with her,' Dane nodded, the satisfaction showing on his face, there because he believed he'd exposed Lily's original claim about his brother as a lie. 'Grandfather was furious because he never liked any of us playing so close to home.'

Lily nodded, making Dane relax a little because it seemed as if she was confirming his brother's masculinity. 'He even threatened to disinherit Daniel if he did anything like it again.'

Again Lily nodded, but this time Dane sighed impatiently. 'So what was wrong with my brother sowing a few wild oats?' he demanded. 'Grandfather may have cursed and sworn a bit about it, but he didn't mean half he had said.'

'But he would have carried out his threat if he'd known the truth,' Lily stated heavily.

'What truth?' he snapped. 'I've just given you the truth! It's you who wants to turn it all into something nasty!'

'The truth, Dane, is that Daniel only wanted to make it look as if he was interested in Sonia! H-he used her that summer, strung her along b-because he didn't want any of you finding out that he was——'

'Don't!' Taking a threatening step towards her, he actually looked as if he was going to strike her. 'Don't so much as imply what you were going to say! Or so help me, Lily, I'll——'

'All right—all right!' she choked, lifting a trembling hand in a soothing gesture. 'Let's just say, then, that Daniel allowed a flirtation to develop between himself and Sonia, then didn't quite know how to back out of it when it was time to go back to college!'

He nodded abruptly, allowing himself to accept that much, if nothing else. And Lily closed her eyes for a moment in an effort to gather her wits. His abrupt surge of violence had shaken her. It showed that he was not as in control of himself as he would like to appear.

'Sh-she followed him to college,' she went on huskily. 'Began haunting the small house he rented with several of us. W-we teased him about it for a while, until she started to be a real nuisance, began linking my name with Daniel's or one of the other two girls who also shared the house. This all happened around the time my mother had taken a serious turn for the worse. She was constantly in and out of hospital, my father was spending as much time as he could with her, and his business was beginning to suffer. I was worried sick about them both.' She swallowed on the anguish that period in her life would always mean to her. 'So I wasn't following events as closely as everyone else. But it soon became obvious that Sonia was beginning to turn nasty—so nasty, in fact, that she attacked one of the girls outside the house one evening, spewing out all kinds of insults and accusations——' Very much the way you do, she wanted to add, but didn't. 'Out of sheer irritation with her, this girl told Sonia brutally just why she was wasting her time on Daniel!'

'No!' he exploded gruffly.

'Yes!' Lily insisted.

Her blue eyes appealed, his glinted with an antipathy that wrenched at her heart. The silence stretched between them and Lily began to tremble again. If she couldn't bring him to accept that what she was telling him was the truth this time, then she knew she would never get another chance.

'Dane—you have to accept it! Sonia did—and threatened to tell your grandfather!'

CHAPTER EIGHT

DANE slammed down his glass with threatening force.

'Oh, he was very discreet!' Lily said, determined that she was not stopping now, not when she'd come this far. 'Daniel was almost manic about it. He was terrified of any of his family finding out! He said you would all disown him if you knew!'

'A Norfolk, queer as a clockwork monkey?' Daniel's harsh mockery ripped down the years to cut into her just as it had done then. 'You have to be joking. They would never understand——'

'Sonia, explain about bloody Sonia!' Dane growled, turning back to the fridge to withdraw another brandy.

Lily watched him empty it into his glass with growing concern. This was wretched enough without Dane getting drunk on brandy. Folding her arms across her chest, she moved away from the door. She felt cold and stiff, her muscles aching with tension. Carefully, she lowered herself into a chair.

'Sh-she turned vicious,' Lily said. 'Talk about beware of a woman scorned!' Her laugh was thick and bitter. 'She went from loving to despising Daniel in no seconds flat! It was then she began making her threats. She was going to tell his precious grandfather—he'd surely pay well to hush up something as sordid as this in the family! It was bad enough having a son who put it about with any women who would have him—without having a grandson who did quite the opposite!'

Dane actually winced, and Lily bit her lips, not realising just how much of Daniel's bitterness she had been feeding into her words.

'Naturally, Daniel asked her what it would cost to shut her up. Believe it or not, he was more concerned by then that the shame might just be enough to see your grandfather off. He had already had two heart attacks, if you remember. And the doctor had warned that the next one could well be fatal.' Which it had been, she recalled. But at least it had not been brought on by anything Daniel had or had not done. 'She took her money and left, but not before she had gone back to the stud and coerced your grandfather into paying up some more money by threatening to tell one of the tabloids how Daniel Norfolk had used her all summer long. She omitted to say just *how* he had used her,' Lily added drily. 'But what she did say was enough to make your grandfather pay up.'

'Glass houses,' Dane murmured.

'What?' Lily glanced frowningly at him.

'The glass house syndrome,' he explained on a brief grim smile. 'My father's—affairs used to make the tabloids sizzle. Grandfather hated it. Hated what it did to my mother. Was ashamed that his own son could behave like that. It got so bad at one time that it even began to affect the company—until Grandfather took back control from my father. He was a playboy,' Dane stated distastefully. 'Right through to the core, and didn't care who of us he embarrassed so long as he had his fun. Daniel and I only survived it because Grandfather kept us firmly under his wing while we were growing up. But he possessed a bitter dislike for scandal of any kind from anyone else. He called it the glass house syndrome. Our father's escapades forced us to live in a glass house where the Press was concerned, and it was up to us to make sure we gave no one the chance to throw any more stones at it.'

Hence Dane's own preference for the kind of well seasoned, sophisticated woman who knew how to play the game, Lily realised. The ones who didn't kiss and tell.

'Well, then, you'll understand better than I thought you would why Daniel was so sure that your grandfather was serious when he threatened to disinherit him if he didn't find a wife.'

Dane nodded. 'But it does not explain why you had to be the one to take on the job.'

'But it will do.' She took a deep breath. Feeling exhausted now, she at least seemed to have managed to defuse Dane's anger. 'I explained how ill my mother was. What I did not add was that in paying the huge medical bills it cost to give her the best care his money could buy my father began to fall into debt.' She shrugged fatalistically. 'Added to that, he had been neglecting his business, delegating more than he should so he could spend as much time with my mother as he could. I'd already discovered his problems and was worrying myself sick wondering how I could help him out. I'd even decided to give up college and get a job— any job if it would help. When I discovered Daniel's problem and he discovered mine, it seemed like the ideal solution that we help each other out. He would bail my father out and I would marry him.' She shrugged. 'It was to be a purely business arrangement. T-to end once your grandfather had— gone.'

She swallowed, then lifted her eyes to Dane's. 'W-we were in the process of getting a divorce when

Daniel was killed,' she told him huskily, deciding she might as well get the whole lot off her chest now she'd started. 'W-which was why I was so horrified by his will. It really wasn't what we'd arranged...'

'He was young, Lily. He can't possibly have expected to have the damned thing read,' Dane suggested.

'Yes,' she whispered, grateful to Dane for not suspecting her of having had an influence in Daniel's decision. It was more than generous of him in the circumstances. 'Anyway...' Wearily now, she lurched back on to their original track. 'We struck a deal. And as far as everyone who mattered was concerned we promised to do our damnedest to make it look like the love-match of the decade. It worked,' she added drily. 'We deceived everyone except for you.'

'Which makes you both—what, I wonder?' Dane drawled cynically.

'What you always suspected us of being, I suppose,' she shrugged. 'A pair of liars—good liars,' she pointed out ruefully. 'But liars all the same.'

'And did you feel any love for him at all, Lily?' he enquired gruffly.

'Oh, yes.' Her smile softened into genuine affection. 'Who couldn't? He was so easy to love. I loved Daniel as a dear, dear friend, as the man who bailed my family out at its final hour.'

'A man,' Dane grunted deridingly.

'Yes, a man!' Lily flared, hating to hear him aim that tone at Daniel. 'He was a good man! A kind, caring man. A man who was prepared to go to any lengths to protect his family from hurt. And don't you dare imply he was anything else!'

'He was a bloody homosexual, Lily!' Dane cried, and in so doing said it all—all that was hurting Dane at any rate.

Lily sighed heavily. 'You don't always get to choose everything you are in your life, Dane,' she pointed out huskily. 'Sometimes the choice is made for you even before you're born.' A smile touched her mouth. Dane didn't see it, but it was full of rueful fatalism because she was thinking of her love for him. That had to have been a decision made for her before she was born, because she was sure she wouldn't have made it if she'd had a choice. 'The knack, so Daniel told me once, is knowing what you do with it once you've got it.'

'*It* being his sexuality,' Dane drawled, seeing no humour in the pun at all.

'*It* being,' Lily patiently corrected, 'his natural warmth, his unfailing sense of humour, his gentle love for anything breathing, whether man or beast—*and* his sexuality! Dane...' She pleaded for understanding, rising from her chair to approach him. 'Where has Daniel changed in your memory of him on discovering his secret? Think about it,' she urged. 'Has his head changed shape? Has he grown an extra limb to make him stand out as something different—strange? Does it make him a lesser person—or less deserving of your love, now you do know?'

'No!' He denied that unassailingly.

'Then it's his love for you, you feel is in question,' she concluded. 'But Dane!' she appealed. 'It was that very love for you which made him hide all of this from you—from all your family! He hated hurting people, you know that! But most of all he could not stand the thought of disappointing you! He worshipped you—looked up to you! You were the person he most wished he could be and knew he could never hope to emulate—even without his homosexuality!'

'I'm nothing special,' Dane muttered, made uncomfortable by the suggestion.

She was standing right beside him now, her gaze fixed on his tension-locked profile. She didn't attempt to touch him; she had a feeling Dane would erupt if she so much as tried it. He was a man in pain, and just like any animal was ready to hit out at the one who caused his pain—namely, herself.

'You're pedestal material, Dane.' Lily smiled, despite the gravity of the subject. 'A man's ideal of a man, Daniel once described you. Good looks, sex

appeal, a natural gift for handling power and a kind
of spiritual charisma which sets you apart from the
lesser mortals. As I said, hard to emulate, and
Daniel didn't even want to try! He loved you for
what you are and despite what you are. You are
you, and Daniel was Daniel.' She shrugged as if
that said it all. 'Two separate individuals who could
laugh, cry, dance, sing—walk, talk, sleep, eat—
feel! Daniel was as big a success in his chosen ca-
reer as you were in yours,' she stated proudly. 'And
in a way, even those careers were not as diverse as
they seemed. You both possessed the ability to ma-
nipulate. In Daniel's case it was horses. In yours it
was people. So, where did you separate? In bed,'
she stated bluntly, and watched Dane wince. 'But
where and on whom Daniel bestowed his sexual
love was a deep and personal thing which had
nothing to do with anyone but Daniel. Being homosexual did not mean that he despised all women
or saw every man as a potential partner. He was
your brother, Dane, and expected to be loved as a
brother should be loved.'

'And did he love you as a wife should be loved,
Lily?'

The cynicism was hard and cutting, and Lily was
feeling limp from her long defence of Daniel. But
she answered him clearly enough. 'I was loved as
this wife wanted to be loved by him—with warmth

and a deep affection. We were happy together, Dane. And no one, not even you with your bitterness, will take that away from us.'

'And his—love for Mark Radley, wasn't that a betrayal of your loyalty to him?' he then asked grimly. 'On marrying you, did my brother then remain faithful to the promises you made to each other?'

'I—I don't know what you mean,' she murmured frowningly.

'Oh, of course you do,' Dane drawled, turning at last to look at her. His eyes were dark, dark and deriding. 'You married my brother to save both our families from a scandal. You put your own personal life on hold for them. Did Daniel and Mark Radley put their personal needs on hold for you?'

She went hot then cold, unable to answer. In all honesty she hadn't looked at things from that angle before. It shocked her to realise that Dane had a very valid point.

'No, of course they didn't,' he taunted cynically. 'I can see the answer written on your lovely face.' Grasping her chin, he lifted it so that she had no choice but to take the full brunt of his bitter contempt. 'They used you, Lily,' he stated brutally. 'They—both of them—used you to their own very comfortable and secure ends.'

'It wasn't like that!' she denied.

'It was exactly like that!' he snapped, letting her go and thrusting his hands angrily into his pockets. 'If there had been one ounce of decency in my brother, he would not have even considered tainting you with his sins!'

'It isn't a sin to——'

'The sin, Lily,' he cut in harshly, 'was in the shame he felt for himself! But did he have to take the only innocent party in it all and taint her, just to save his own worthless neck?'

'I needed Daniel's help as much as he needed mine,' Lily pointed out.

'Your father would have pulled through without your intervention, Lily,' Dane derided that, too. 'He's riding high on his success again now, isn't he?'

She nodded, unable to argue with that. 'And he paid Daniel back every penny he loaned him,' she felt constrained to add.

Dane nodded, briefly, his stern face satisfied. 'And Daniel should have come to me,' he then added gruffly. 'Showed a bit of spunk and come to me—trusted me enough to confide in me, and asked me to sort Sonia out!'

'Would you—could you have done?' she asked jerkily.

'I'd have had a bloody good try,' he muttered.

'And despised Daniel for the rest of his life,' she choked.

'Maybe,' Dane admitted, 'I don't know.' Wearily he lifted a hand to his neck, rubbing it tensely. 'I wasn't given the opportunity to find out, was I?'

No. Lily wilted back into a chair. Dane had been given no chance, no trust. It only occurred to her then just how unjustly he had been used.

'And Radley,' he muttered. 'What was he thinking while all of this was going on?'

She sucked in a deep breath, her heavy lungs heaving on it. 'He never liked any of it,' she confessed. Hence the urgent conversations over cups of coffee before she and Daniel got married. 'He—he always did want Daniel to tell you. He believed that you loved Daniel enough to take it.'

'So one of you at least had faith in me.'

Lily lowered her head in shame. 'He was of the firm opinion that not only could you help soothe your grandfather away from this marriage idea he'd decided upon, but you would perhaps, if you were appealed to, help m-my father through his difficulties too. B-but Daniel refused to take the risk of losing your love and respect and I—well——' she shrugged emptily '—I'd already met you by then and...'

She didn't need to say any more. He knew what she'd thought. He'd frightened her to death on sight with the violence of her own attraction to him.

'You still should not have married him, Lily.' As if reading her thoughts, Dane looked at her grimly. 'All you did by marrying my brother despite what you felt for me was put us both through two long years of hell. It could have been different with a bit of trust—a whole lot bloody different. God,' he sighed. 'I've got to get out of here before I——' He spun abruptly for the door.

'But—where are you going?' Lily jumped agitatedly to her feet.

'God knows,' he muttered. 'As far away from all of—this as I can get!'

'But Dane!' She rushed after him. 'You aren't fit to be going anywhere!' He was in shock though he probably didn't recognise it. 'Please . . .' She grabbed hold of his arm, feeling the muscles bunch and tremble beneath her clutching fingertips. 'Stay here with me.'

'For God's sake, Lily,' he ground out tautly. 'Can't you understand? I can't take any more right now!'

'And I leave tomorrow,' she reminded him thickly. 'If you feel anything for me at all, then you just can't leave like this, now!'

He stared down at her for a long moment, that look of hell still glowing in his eyes. He knew what she was asking, knew also what it was doing to her to beg him like this.

'Don't ask more of me than I can give, Lily,' he rasped.

More than he could give? Did that mean that what they'd shared before this thing with Daniel had blown up had been enough for him? It had been the most wonderful experience of her life, and he was dismissing it as enough!

Something winced inside her, and she let go of his arm, turning her back on him so that he wouldn't see the pain in her eyes. Her arms locked like steel bands around her aching body while she waited for him to walk out of the door—and out of her life forever.

There was a muffled sound behind her, and she stiffened jerkily in readiness for the final slamming of the door. But it didn't come. Instead, she felt his arms snake angrily around her, and in the next moment she was being turned, lifted off the floor, and her mouth assaulted by a kiss that knocked the breath from her body as he carried her back to the bed.

Lily let him do his worst to her. Let him drag her, weak and helpless, through uncharted planes of beautiful sensation. The depth of sensuality a body could generate astonished her. And her response to it seemed to inspire him to greater things.

By the time the grey light of morning came creeping into the room, Lily lay beside his deeply sleeping form, feeling utterly sated, every last one of her veils of innocence wrenched clean away. And she made herself face what she was leaving behind her in a few short hours.

After all, what would she be gaining if she decided to stay here? she asked herself as that temptation began playing tantalisingly on her mind. A week, a month—maybe, if she was lucky, several months of immersing herself in this kind of exquisite torment?

And don't forget the sneaking about while they enjoyed it, she reminded herself grimly. Neither Dane's nor her own pride would take the public lashing an open affair between the two of them would create.

She was his brother's new widow. And nothing would alter the sense of utter distaste people would feel if they ever discovered they were together like this.

Don't ask more of me than I can give, he'd said. And she wouldn't.

By hanging on to every last thread of her determination, she felt she could probably walk away from him without revealing to him just how much of herself she would be leaving behind.

Quietly, carefully so as not to wake him, she eased herself out of the bed and gathered together her clothes before tiptoeing into the bathroom where she showered quickly, dressed herself in the neat clouded-blue silk-mix suit she'd set aside to travel in, then sneaked quietly back into the bedroom, hoping to get away before Dane realised she'd gone——

Then stopped dead on the threshold of the room, when she found him up and already dressed, sitting waiting for her on the neatly made bed.

'Oh,' she said, disconcerted. He needed a shave, was her next incomprehensible thought. The dark shadow of a long night's growth was lying darkly against his skin.

'Leaving without bothering with any breakfast, Lily?' he drawled sarcastically.

She didn't know what to say. She had hoped to get away without this kind of confrontation. It had been essential to her own sanity that she do so. Now? Wryly, she accepted the prospect of yet more pain. More anguish. And, composing her features, she faced him squarely. 'I was going to snatch a bite at the airport,' she answered. 'I—I d-didn't want to wake you, so I was just going to order a taxi and...'

Her voice trailed off, curtailed by the expression in his eyes. It was hard and cold, and bitterly cynical.

Neither moved, neither spoke, and gradually, as the silence slowly closed them in, the very air around them began to hum.

What he was thinking she did not know—what he *wanted* from her she didn't know either. He was certainly mulling something over in his mind as he sat there, mouth pulled into a thin, tight line. Considering whether or not to ask her to stay? she wondered. Deciding whether the effort was worth it or not? He'd lusted after her body for a long time. Now he'd had it, tasted it, slaked himself with it. But had he slaked himself enough to let her go?

'I'll take you,' he said quietly at last.

Enough. He'd had enough.

Her heart flapped sickeningly in her breast. Feeling her face go pale, she let her eyes drop away from his. What had she expected? she asked herself bitterly. Vows of undying love?

And she'd had enough too, hadn't she?

'No,' she heard herself say, and wondered dizzily just what she was saying no to—his offer or her own wretched thoughts. 'It—it's all right. I'd rather——'

'I said I'd take you!' The fury burst from nowhere, making her start. 'I'll take you, dammit,' he repeated roughly. 'I'll bloody take you.' And he got up abruptly. 'Just give me a moment to freshen up.' Grimly he pushed by her and went into the bathroom, shutting the door behind him.

Shaking with reaction, she glanced fleetingly at the telephone standing so temptingly on the bedside cabinet. Did she have time to call Reception and get out of here before he——?

But no. Ruefully, she sank down into one of the chairs. She had a bill to settle, her luggage to have taken down. Where she'd even got the crazy idea she could just creep out of here this morning without Dane knowing was beyond her, now she had time to think about it.

'Crazy just about says it,' she mumbled drily to herself.

He came back, looking much more like the man she was used to seeing with his jaw freshly shaved. It was the kind of hotel which supplied complimentary necessities for the caught-out guest. Dane had certainly been caught out, she mused wryly— virtually jumped on by her twice and begged to stay.

She shuddered, despising herself now in the cold light of day for behaving like that. And got up, giving herself something to do by gathering up the evidence of her overnight stay and pushing it into her flight bag.

'Ready?' He had his key dangling from restless fingers. His expression about as approachable as iced rock.

She nodded mutely. He went and picked up her two suitcases.

'Can you manage that?' He nodded grimly at the flight bag.

She nodded her reply, too choked inside to speak. And without another word they left the room.

They didn't speak on their way down in the lift either. And the tension between them was shocking. We've been here before, Lily recognised wryly.

By the time they were in the car and driving, the air between them was suffocating. She sat stiffly beside him, barely daring to breathe in case it set off the explosion she knew was waiting to erupt between them.

Twice on that short, grimly silent journey Dane pulled the car into the side of the road and stopped. And each time Lily tensed herself ready for whatever he was going to throw at her—only to feel the tension increase when, after a few minutes of it, and without saying a single word, he pulled back into the road and continued their journey.

She was wilting beneath the strain when they eventually arrived at the airport. Dane switched off the engine, made her start violently when he reached across her to open up the glove compartment; she saw his mouth compress even further at her uncontrolled reaction, watched him withdraw a black leather wallet then climb grimly out of the car.

She wished he hadn't, wished he'd just remained in his seat silent and grim, waited for her to climb out then shot off into the distance, never to be seen or heard of again. It would have been much easier for her that way. But then, Dane had never made anything easy for her, she remembered as she followed him out of the car, then stood waiting while he found a trolley and stacked her luggage on it.

'I won't come any further,' he clipped, not looking at her but at some unspecified something on the airport building.

'I... Right,' she said. 'Fine. I'll...' God, this was worse than she'd thought it was going to be. Tears were making her throat ache. 'Thank you,' she finished numbly.

'Don't write. Don't call.' His clipped voice stung. 'Don't so much as try to get in touch with me for the next six months—— Six months, Lily,' he repeated tightly.

Then he was gone, striding back to his car and climbing in, driving away without so much as looking at her fully in the face.

Six months, she was repeating dazedly to herself. What was she supposed to do with the next six months? She stood there, gripping on to the luggage trolley because it was the only solid thing holding her up, having to fight the will to grab a cab and go after him.

But what would she be going to? Dane was not and never would be hers to keep. Oh, he talked about time, and waiting. But they both knew why they had snatched at last night. It had been now or never, because once distance and time had separated them he would soon go back to his old, comfortably uncommitted ways, his desire and curiosity for her abating once she was thoroughly out of his life.

She'd loved him almost from the beginning while he had only lusted. There was no future in that.

CHAPTER NINE

IT WAS a lovely night. Lily stood on the deck which spanned the back of her parent's home, her thighs resting against the veranda rail. Her bare arms were folded across the bodice of the raspberry silk cocktail dress she was wearing, and she gazed out across the bay at the famous Sydney Harbour Bridge—a view she had gazed on like this often over the last few months, when the need for a few minutes' escape from the busy social life her parents had determinedly built up around her became essential to her remaining sane.

The air smelled sweet of jasmine, and a light breeze played gently on the surface of the aquamarine water of their subtly lit swimming-pool. There was a full moon above, the velvet dark sky studded with stars. And behind her the sound of light after-dinner conversation filtered out towards her through the open patio doors.

She inhaled slowly then let the breath out again, enjoying the sheer peace and tranquillity of the moment. Her parents had become so content here that they had decided to stay. Buy this beautiful house. Settle.

Mark too seemed content—or as content as he ever could be being who and what he was—to remain in Hong Kong. She had spent a couple of weeks with him there only a month ago. He was beginning to pick up the threads of his life again, get over Daniel. Aided, she didn't doubt, by the instant success his paintings had been there.

But she missed England. She missed the sheer greenness of it, the narrow, wet lanes where high flanking hedgerows sparkled from a heavy downpour of rain. She missed the misty fall of dew on a cool autumn evening. And hot summer days where a light breeze always managed to keep the air cool enough to breathe—unlike here, she smiled to herself, feeling the humidity in the air like a wet cloth to her scantily covered skin.

And she missed Dane—— Oh, not as she missed everything else England meant to her. No, she missed Dane with a physical ache that sometimes held her paralysed in its grip, whereas the other things were an innate yearning, bred into her genes as the place her heart knew as home.

Dane did not represent home. Dane represented danger, fire, passion and pain. He represented uncertainty, risk, and the promise of her having to endure the bitter taste of loss a second time around.

Dane. Her heart shook, sending the breath from her lungs on a shaky sigh. The longer she had been away from him, the more convinced she had become that it was better to stay away. She didn't think she could survive the emotional trauma of loving and losing him a second time. She'd barely scraped through the last one.

And it was the lying again. Lies she was heartsick of living with. Here, she was poor Mrs Lily Norfolk, the tragic young widow. Oh, she missed Daniel—of course she did. But only as one would miss a dear, dear friend. The real grieving for Daniel was Mark's prerogative, which he did in quiet solitude while he painted.

Sometimes she wished she had an excuse to just hide away the way Mark could. At least alone she could grieve with honesty, for herself, and what could never be.

Then there were her parents, so loving, so kind, believing her to be so devastated by Daniel's death that they treated her like precious porcelain when really, if they knew the truth, they would most probably be shocked.

And Dane. What would they think of her relationship with Dane?

An affair, with Daniel's brother? she could just hear them gasp. But Lily, that's—that's indecent! Think what everyone would suspect—say!

'Glass houses,' she muttered deridingly, realising that she too had her own glass house to protect. 'Bloody glass houses.'

So she hadn't told them about Dane. And that lie festered along with all the other lies she'd cultivated over the years.

She could, if she remained here, build a nice, clean, comfortable life for herself. She'd made a whole new circle of friends here. Nice people— people who took her as she was and did not expect more of her than she was able to give, which was fortunate, she conceded drily, because the ability to give much of herself seemed to have been sapped completely out of her.

Dane had done that. He had taken all she had in her to give and left her stripped of the ability to feel anything else deeply—or *want* to feel deeply, which was nearer the truth. Her parents had noticed it, though they had not tried talking to her about it— which was a good job because she didn't know if she could change the quiet, almost withdrawn attitude she'd brought here with her to Australia.

It was as if she'd once again put her life on hold for the benefit of other people. Maybe she would go all the way through her life suppressing her own needs and desires for others, she mused heavily. Maybe that was her karma.

'Planning your escape?'

Automatically a smile came to her lips as she turned her head to watch her father come out of the house and walk across the deck to come and lean beside her.

'You looked so wistful,' he explained his mocking remark. 'As if something way out there——' he gave a nod of his blond head out into the twinkling ocean '—was drawing you.'

'England,' she nodded, 'I'm missing England.' But it was Dane's harshly attractive features which swam up in front of her mind.

'Ah,' he sighed. 'The Aussies aren't civilised enough for you. I should have known it.'

Lily laughed. 'They're about as civilised, cosmopolitan and sophisticated as the rest of the Western world, Daddy, and you know it! They just enjoy teasing us with their cork-hatted, beer-swilling, saddle-swaggering image, that's all.'

He grinned, enjoying her witty sarcasm, then murmured quietly, 'But if everyone is so civilised, sophisticated and cosmopolitan, why are you hankering for England?'

'Home,' she corrected. 'I'm—hankering, as you put it, for home.'

'So, when are you leaving?'

'Maybe I don't want to leave,' she shrugged, then smiled up at him. 'A girl can be a little homesick without wanting to catch the next plane out of here, can't she?'

His brows cocked mockingly at her. 'Even when she's been just about itching to leave here from the moment she landed?'

Lily looked away, unable to hold his stare.

'How long have you been here, Lily?' he asked quietly.

'Six months,' she answered, and without having to think about it. Six long and empty——

'Been counting the days, have you?' he teased.

She flushed, realising just how quickly her answer had tripped off her tongue. 'I've been very happy here, Daddy.' Irritation at his perception put a slight snap to her voice.

'So happy in fact,' he drawled, 'that I have yet to see you smile with your beautiful blue eyes—or accept a second date from the steady stream of men who've slipped hopefully in and sadly out of your life since you came here.'

'I've just lost my husband,' she reminded him curtly.

His brief nod acknowledged that. 'But giving some of these hopeful chaps the chance to help you get over him would not go against the international laws of decency, Lily.'

Decency? She almost laughed at the word. Her poor father, for all his worldly sophistication, would be shocked at his daughter's low level of decency! And anyway, she thought acidly, the decency line was drawn at six months—exactly—Dane had personally drawn it. And she had only just reached it.

'I'm not ready for anything heavy,' she said.

'Heavy?' he repeated, then he sighed and settled his hand gently over her own. 'Lily,' he said, 'Daniel was a wonderful man, and you loved each other very much. But don't you think it's time you let him go?'

Oh, God. She closed her eyes on the well of shamed tears. Lies compounding on lies. 'I will,' she whispered. 'When I'm ready.' Thinking of Dane—as always, thinking of Dane. 'Look...' She couldn't stand this any more. 'I'm tired. I think I'm going to turn in for the night. Tell Mummy goodnight for me.' With a quick brush of her lips against his cheek she escaped to her own room before she said something she really would regret.

The trouble was, she analysed her own tension as she prepared for bed, Dane filled her mind. Dane and the six months she had apart from him. Six very specific months that were over as from today. And she had a hard struggle ahead of her deciding what she was going to do!

'Oh, hell,' she murmured as she sat down wearily on the side of her bed.

On impulse she picked up the telephone, dialling the international number of perhaps the only person in this world she felt she could talk more freely with.

Mark answered almost immediately. 'Did I get you out of bed?' she asked when she'd listened to his yawning greeting.

'At——' he must have glanced at his watch '—nine o'clock in the evening?' he mocked. 'I'm not in my dotage yet, Lily.'

'You were yawning,' she accused.

'I was stretching my aching back!' he corrected. 'If you must know, you've stopped me working.'

'Painting,' she assumed.

'Painting, yes,' he agreed. 'But with one of those brushes that sloshes the stuff on walls. I'm decorating my apartment.'

'Oh,' she laughed, beginning to feel better just simply talking to him.

'So, what's up?' She heard him making himself comfortable, and did the same herself, curling up on her bed with the phone resting on her pillow by her ear.

'Nothing,' she said evasively. 'I—just felt like ringing you, that's all.'

'At...' he did the quick three-hour adjustment of time between Sydney and Hong Kong '...midnight? On a Friday night? Long-distance?' he mocked.

'Mmm,' she murmured non-committally.

Silence, while he digested the suspect reply. 'Fed up?' he suggested.

'Mmm,' she murmured again.

'Of Sydney or the lazy life you lead there?'

'Both,' she said. 'I think I want to go home.'

'Then why don't you?'

Logical question, Lily supposed. It was a shame she couldn't give him a logical answer to it.

'The stud will still be there, waiting for you,' Mark continued when she said nothing. 'All you have to do is walk back in the door and—hey presto!—home.'

'No. Not the stud.' The stud would never be home to her again. 'You know I never wanted it. I don't even understand why Daniel had to leave it to me. It only caused me more problems.'

'He left it to you because he wanted to know you would be taken care of,' Mark stated flatly. 'And the only reason that causes you problems is because of Dane Norfolk.'

'Dane?' she repeated guardedly. 'What does he have to do with anything?'

'Everything, I should imagine,' Mark said drily. 'He always was your tormentor—and you his,' he added carefully.

'You know as well as I do that Dane and I barely spoke to one another!'

'You didn't dare,' he mocked. 'It was bad enough when your eyes met. The room shook. If you'd said more than two words to each other the walls would have come tumbling down. Daniel used to worry himself over it because he knew you were no match against his brother's famous prowess.'

'Don't be ridiculous!' she snapped, wishing she hadn't made this telephone call. The trouble with Mark was he had always been too damned perceptive for her own good.

'Is it ridiculous to wonder why he came flying all the way out here six months ago just to find out what the hell had been going on between the three of us?' he drawled.

'You never told me that before!' Lily sat up abruptly, suddenly all jumping nerves. 'When— when did he go to see you?' she demanded breathlessly. Mark hadn't so much as mentioned this when she'd visited him last month! But then, she conceded, she had told him nothing either. In fact they'd both avoided so much as mentioning Dane's name.'

'Just after you flew out to Sydney,' Mark revealed.

Lily flopped back on her pillows, her stomach tying itself in knots. 'What did he want?' she breathed, not sure she really wanted to know.

'Well, he certainly didn't come for his health,' Mark said drily. 'In fact, I'd say the man was suffering. Suffering from a lot of things,' he added provokingly, 'but the main one being a burning need to come to terms with what his brother was.'

'Oh.' The following silence was heavy. 'Was— was he cruel to you, Mark?' Lily questioned huskily, her teeth worrying at her bottom lip. She knew from painful experience how nasty Dane could be when he didn't like something.

And he hadn't liked what he'd discovered his brother to be.

'No,' Mark denied, then sighed quietly. 'If anything he was—sad. Sad that Daniel hadn't felt able to tell him himself. Sad because he'd discovered that he didn't really know his brother at all. And he wanted to know,' he added gruffly, 'everything I could tell him. How did he manage to get the truth out of you, Lily?' he then asked curiously. 'Because if there's one thing I'm sure about where Dane Norfolk is concerned, he did not use fair means, and most probably used foul—had to have done to make you tell him everything!'

'I…we argued.' She hedged restlessly around the truth. 'Over Daniel's will, and he sort of—angered the truth out of me.'

'Seduced it out of you, more like,' Mark scoffed.

'That's not true!' she denied, guilty red flooding into her cheeks because it was so damned true that she began to wonder if Dane had told Mark how it happened! 'And anyway—this was all over months ago, so why have you suddenly decided to bring it all up now?'

'Dane Norfolk,' Mark replied. 'And the fact that all your restlessness and uncertainty is down to him. You're in love with him, aren't you?'

'Oh, God.' Lily covered her eyes, unable to go on denying it any longer. Sick of denying it. Sick of the continuing round of lies she was still having to tell. Sick of the whole damned thing.

Mark's voice came gentle but gruff down the line to her. 'I must assume by your reaction that there is no hope for you with him?'

'Oh—there's hope!' Lily said bitterly. 'One can always cling on to hope! But the real question is whether or not I want to take a chance with him on such a tenuous thing as hope!'

And she told him, quietly, flatly. She told him everything, leaving nothing out.

'Your six months are up,' he noted when she'd finished.

'Yes,' she sighed.

'And ... ?' Mark prompted.

'And nothing,' she shrugged. 'I don't think I have it in me to walk into a life of never knowing, of waiting for the hammer to fall, of watching for the signs that will tell me he's tiring of me the way he eventually does of all his women.' Another helpless shrug, and a bitter wry twist to her mouth to go with it. 'If I really thought that there was even a small chance that he might learn to love me, I'd go back to him like a shot!'

'But it isn't love Dane wants from you,' Mark said for her.

'No.' It was sex—sex all the way.

'Didn't some clever devil once say that it was better to have loved and lost than never to have loved at all?' Mark said musingly.

'And is it?' she threw sharply back.

'Oh, yes,' he sighed. 'Infinitely better—though I hope to God I don't meet up with it again in this lifetime. One lot of loving memories are more than enough to cope with, believe me.'

That was no help, Lily thought heavily. What he had just given her with one hand Mark had quickly taken back with the other!

'If you want my advice, Lily,' Mark concluded grimly, 'then it's go for it. Go for it with all you've got, or you'll only spend the rest of your life wondering just what you actually passed up.'

And she considered it, considered it very seriously over the ensuing days. But every time the decision to go back to London and take her chances became almost impossible to resist, she would take time to pause and wonder just what she would be going back to—Dane welcoming her with open, loving arms? Or Dane lost in the arms of another woman, showing Lily that his six months had not been wasted the way hers had been?

And then there were those glass houses—those damned glass houses which said that, even if he did still want her, in the eyes of the world it would still be wrong.

Six months was not long enough. A year was only marginally better. And perhaps there never would be a stretch of time long enough to make any relationship between them both acceptable.

She let the decision drift for a few more days— days when her quietness and preoccupation became a concern to her parents. So much of a concern that she began spending more time out of the house, walking the beautiful stretch of beach below their house, alone, brooding, wishful, afraid.

Then, two weeks to the day after her six-month deadline, and just as she had made the firm decision to write to Dane and tell him that she was going to remain here in Sydney with her family, something happened to turn that decision right on its head.

She'd been for yet another long walk along the beach in an effort to sort her tangled feelings out. And she was tired, hot and thirsty when she came back into the house, intending to make directly for the kitchen for a long glass of something cool then up to her room for a shower before she tackled her dratted letter—when her father stopped her in the hallway.

'I've got something for you,' he said, and beckoned her into the study he had converted into a makeshift office from which he dealt with his business interests in London as well the ones he now had here in Sydney. 'Here,' he said, picking up an A4 sheet of paper from his desk and handing it to her. 'It came through on my fax machine just ten minutes ago. What the hell does it mean, Lily?' he demanded frowningly.

Frowning herself, she looked down at the sheet. Then went pale, her fingers beginning to tremble as she read the message written in large, scrawling print across it.

'Where the hell are you, Lily? Come home!' it said, nothing else. But the words were underlined by the deep, scoring lines of an angry pen.

Trembling, she sank into a chair, her eyes blurring with weak, pathetic tears. Home, he'd called it. And something like a dam split right open inside her to let a whole river of desperate longing wash over her.

'Well?' her father demanded. 'What is it? Who is it from?'

'Dane,' she whispered. 'It's from Dane.'

'Norfolk?' Her father sounded utterly confounded. 'Norfolk's ordering you back to England?'

No, he's ordering me home, Lily corrected silently. Home.

But home to what? The uncertainties began to niggle at her again. Home to the bitter-sweet torment of a one-sided love? Home to accepting the barely veiled insinuations of others—or the careful disguising of what they were doing? Home to yet more lies, more deception?

Glass houses—glass houses! Those bloody glass houses!

'M-may I send back a reply?' she asked her father.

'Of course,' he said, still looking completely bemused. 'Help yourself. But I can't think why he's so eager to get you back. Trouble with Daniel's estate, do you think? Or with the stud maybe? You always did run that place like a well oiled engine,

Lily,' he blustered on, regardless of her trembling impatience. 'Bet it can't run efficiently without you now.'

'I—yes.' Lily wasn't listening. 'Do you mind if I do it—now?' Shakily she came back to her feet.

'What? Oh. Yes, of course.' Her father frowned at her, then shrugged and walked quickly out of the room.

The moment he'd gone Lily darted around his desk to search for a pen. 'Glass houses,' she muttered to herself as she laid the fax sheet down on the desk and scrawled her reply across it in letters just as sharply etched as his had been.

'What about the glass houses?' she demanded. Then she turned and fed the paper back into the fax, stabbed in the return-fax number, firmly hit the 'send' button. Then, while the machine went about the job it was designed for, she sat down heavily again—feeling as if she'd just climbed Mount Everest without a stop.

Silence. The room hit her with it. The machine hit her with it. Even her pounding heart had taken on the beat of a silent drum.

She waited. The minutes ticked agonisingly by. How long did it take to send a fax and receive a reply, for God's sake? What if Dane wasn't there? What if he'd just sent his rotten summons then gone out, arrogantly certain of her obedience? What if——?

The machine kicked into life. So did Lily, jerking out of her seat to go and stand over it anxiously, watching as it fed out a fresh sheet of paper.

Only it was fresh but not fresh—a clean sheet littered with their previous messages, his a grimly etched command, hers a sharply struck reply. Then the new words—words which brought new tears rushing to her eyes.

'To hell with the glass houses!' they said. 'I need you. Come home!'

Her heart flipped. Her stomach did the same. She began to laugh—laugh so uncontrollably that even she recognised that she was verging on a fit of hysterics. But it was as though a huge pressing weight had been lifted from her shoulders because Dane had said to hell with the glass houses, and suddenly nothing else seemed to matter any more. It didn't matter what people wanted to say about them! It didn't even matter that he'd used the word 'need' instead of 'love'! At least he'd said 'need'— that had to mean something—didn't it?

'Coming home,' she printed boldly, and fed the paper back into the machine, waited until it had finished sending her message then snatched the A4 sheet up and pressed it lovingly to her breast.

It was the closest thing she'd ever had to a love-letter, and, madly scrawled on and barely legible as it was, she would cherish it till the day she died!

London was cold and damp, the sky heavily laden with threat of yet more rain to come. Lily shivered inside her thin jacket of taupe linen which had seemed perfectly adequate to travel in when she'd left the blazing heat of Sydney behind her. Now, and even with the efficient heating system in Heathrow airport, she felt chilled, perhaps not helped by the dragging sense of tiredness her long journey had left her with.

No stop-over this time. She had come home to Dane direct.

He was supposed to meet her. And her stomach fluttered nervously as she turned the corner out of Customs then paused, staring blankly at the wall of faces that met her. Perhaps he wouldn't come per-sonally, she thought suddenly. Perhaps he would send Jo-Jo. After all, he might say to hell with the glass houses, but he had been quick to leave her at the airport six months ago, and that could only mean he was reluctant to be seen in public with——

She saw him. The flutters in her stomach be-came an avalanche. He was standing slightly apart from everyone else, his eyes fixed on her, his lean face held in a grim, hard mask.

No welcoming smile. Lily felt her hands slip on the handle of the luggage trolley she was clinging to, nervous sweat breaking out all over her. Mouth dry, heart thumping, she made herself move forward, her eyes never leaving the hard penetration of his silver-grey ones.

'Hi,' she murmured huskily, restraint showing itself in the way her smile barely appeared before it was gone again.

He didn't attempt to smile back. 'You're late,' he clipped out instead.

'No,' she denied, then uncomfortably, 'Well, maybe a little late. Half an hour over time isn't bad when you've come so far...'

His eyes raked quickly over her, and she began to tingle from head to toe, waiting—hoping he was going to take her in his arms——

She tried smiling up at him again, encouraging him to show that he was pleased to see her. But he didn't. If anything he went even more cold-faced. And suddenly all the wonderful excitement she'd carried with her around half the world began to seep quietly out of her.

'C-can we go now?' she asked a little desperately, wondering if it was to be her fate to always be bursting into tears in front of him.

'Of course.' Shifting his cool gaze to somewhere over Lily's left shoulder, he gave a curt nod.

Immediately a hand appeared to grip the loaded trolley in between her own two clutching hands. She glanced up to find Jo-Jo's dearly familiar smile beaming down on her, and at last gave the tears freedom to plug her eyes. 'Jo-Jo,' she laughed, and, unable to resist it, leaned over to hug him to her like a long-lost friend.

'Welcome back, Miss Lily,' he grinned when she let him go again. 'You're a sight for sore old eyes, I can tell you——'

'Let's go,' a curt voice interrupted, and even the small amount of pleasure she'd received from Jo-Jo's warm welcome seeped shiveringly away.

Frowning slightly, Jo-Jo took the trolley from her and turned it to forge a way through the crowds towards the exit. Lily followed numbly behind with Dane walking stiffly at her side. Someone jostled by them, and Dane's arm shot out behind her, protecting her from being bumped. Suddenly she was breathlessly aware of the superior height and width of him, the overwhelming sense of his power and strength, the scent of him, the innate sensuality of him. Heat ran through her like a fire-flash, and ended up crowding 10self into her cheeks.

Then the arm dropped away again, and the fire went out abruptly, leaving her feeling lost and cold, wondering bewilderedly just what she was doing here.

The black limousine was parked as usual on double yellow lines, an ominous-looking slip of paper sandwiched between the windscreen and the wiper. Jo-Jo pushed the trolley towards the boot, and Dane reached past her to open the rear door of the car. She slipped inside without his help, and edged over to the furthest corner of the car, refusing to look at him as he got in beside her.

She felt like crying. She felt like screaming like a fishwife. She felt like crawling into the gutter to hide her bitter sense of hurt and disappointment at his cold attitude towards her.

Sighing heavily, as if he too was unhappy with the whole damned meeting, he sat back in the seat and watched Jo-Jo come around the car, flip out the parking ticket from behind the wiper, open the car door and climb into the driver's seat, tossing the ticket aside as though it was nothing special. He glanced in his mirror, smiled warmly at Lily, frowned blackly at Dane, then set them moving with the tension inside the car enough to suffocate all of them.

It was raining outside. And Lily was feeling the difference in the chill air from what she had been used to in Australia—though she would rather die than tell that to the man sitting so aloofly beside her. She had no idea where he was taking her. It could be to the apartment. It could be to the stud. Or it could even be to Timbuktu for all she found she cared—so long as he did it quickly.

But it became obvious after thirty minutes of them driving amid this stiff-necked silence that he was taking her to the apartment. And suddenly Lily found she didn't want to go anywhere near it!

'Any hotel will do,' she muttered as a heavily loaded hint.

'Will it?' he clipped. And that was it. Discussion over.

The car swept into the car park of his luxury apartment block. Jo-Jo brought them to a smooth halt right outside the entrance, and Dane was out and around to her side before she'd even had chance to open her own door. His fingers bit as he helped her out, and she tugged angrily against them without it making an ounce of difference as he pulled her through the doors and into the waiting lift.

CHAPTER TEN

'WHAT'S the matter with you?' she burst out angrily as he let go of her so abruptly that she almost stumbled.

'Not a bloody thing is wrong with me,' he grunted, and stabbed a hard finger at the lift button. The lift doors slid shut. Dane spun around to face her, and the first trickles of alarm went slithering down Lily's spine when she read the blind fury on his face.

'But what I would like to know,' he uttered tightly, 'is what the hell you were trying to do to me by going two damned weeks over our deadline!'

She blinked and couldn't think of a single thing to say in her defence.

'What was it, Lily?' he rasped. 'A deliberate ploy to make me beg before you were satisfied you'd got me right where you wanted me?'

'Beg?' she gasped. 'You issued a royal command, Dane! I don't find that even remotely close to begging!'

'Well, it was a darn sight closer to begging than anything I received from you!'

The lift doors opened and he stalked out, leaving her standing there staring at the spot he had just vacated, a slow dawning of just what was going on here beginning to make sense in her mind.

Good God, his pride was dented because he had been the first one to break the six-month silence! It had never occurred to her that it could have actually diminished his standing in his own eyes to be the one to make the first move.

But it did now. And the more she thought about it, the angrier she became! So, it was all right for her to do the crawling back. It was all right if it was her pride put on the line—just so long as the great Dane Norfolk's colossal ego wasn't put at risk!

She almost fell out of the lift in her eagerness to confront him. The apartment door swung open on its hinges. She found him in his lounge, standing there with a brandy glass in his hand.

'Is that what that—ice-cold reception at the airport was about?' she demanded, coming to an angry stop on the threshold of the room.

His glance seared her with contempt over the jet-black rim of his lashes. 'Perhaps I thought the next move should come from you,' he suggested deridingly.

Lily gasped, her blue eyes filling her face with incredulity. 'But I made the next move!' she claimed. 'I caught the very next flight out of Sydney back to you!'

'Two weeks late.'

'Oh.' Lily really did not want to go into the whys and wherefores of her two heart-searching and found-lacking weeks. 'I—had a lot to think about.'

'And six months to think about them,' he drawled.

'I wasn't sure you'd still want me to come back,' she confessed.

'Or wasn't sure whether you wanted to come back to me?'

She shifted uncomfortably on the truth. 'I—I was afraid.'

'What—of me?' He looked so stunned that she almost found it in her to laugh. Of course she was afraid of him. She'd always been afraid of him! He had the power to make or break her—wouldn't anyone under that kind of threat be afraid?

'Of what I was going to come back to,' she corrected.

'So you decided it wasn't worth taking the trouble.'

The lift whirred. Lily glanced back along the hall, feeling a sinking sense of relief when Jo-Jo appeared with her luggage. It saved her having to answer that one.

'I'll put these in your old room, shall I, Miss Lily?'

'Er—yes, thank you,' she answered dully. She had expected to be unpacking in Dane's bedroom, with the eager anticipation of sharing his bed with him.

Jo-Jo grimaced at the tension still splitting the air between the other two as he passed by them.

'Drink?'

She glanced back at Dane. He was looking less the angry bull now, though no more approachable.

'I—no, thank you,' she refused. Her time-clock was all up the creek, and to her it was breakfast time, not early evening. 'I would much rather have a shower and change. Dane——' she then appealed anxiously.

'Go and get your shower, Lily,' he cut in heavily, turning his back on her in a way which could only be a dismissal—and a rejection of the apology she was going to make him.

Jo-Jo was just lining up her two suitcases on the ottoman at the bottom of the bed. He glanced up when she came into the room, saw the heavy droop of her body and grimaced ruefully at it.

'Want me to unpack for you, Miss Lily?' he offered.

'No—no, I'll do it myself, thank you,' she refused—then glanced up, frowning at something that had not been quite right about what he'd said. 'Why the change in my title, Jo-Jo?' she asked. 'Not that I mind, of course,' she hastened to add in case he thought he'd offended her. 'But you never used to refer to me as Miss Lily before.'

He shrugged his wiry shoulders. 'Boss's instructions,' he explained. '"No more Mrs Norfolk when she comes," he said. So——' another shrug '—it had to be Miss Lily, didn't it?'

'Just plain Lily would be nice,' she murmured absently.

Why had Dane forbidden Jo-Jo to call her Mrs Norfolk? Because he didn't like her to have the same name as him? Because it reminded him too much of Daniel? Because it made too glaringly clear what their original relationship had been— that of brother- and sister-in-law—and that would challenge those bloody glass houses?

'What's the matter with him, Jo-Jo?' she sighed. 'Why is he behaving like a——?'

'Boor, would suit him best,' Jo-Jo put in for her, smiling grimly. 'He's been under a lot of strain recently,' he explained. 'Which probably explains it best.'

'Business problems?' she asked worriedly, feeling a sudden anxious concern for Dane where a moment ago she'd only felt like throttling him. Poor Dane, she thought, worried about business and all she could do was——

'More like the stressful business of being in love,' he grinned, and walked out of the room.

In love?

Lily stood by the bed feeling as if someone had just walked up to her and punched her hard in her solar plexus. Dane in love? In love with whom?

She began to shake, an aching anguish welling up inside her like a storm, burning at her eyes, her throat, wrapping a band of suffocating pain around her chest and tightening it ruthlessly.

With Judy? With some other exquisitely sophisticated creature Lily had no hope of competing with?

Who could it be? What was she like? Why had he encouraged her to come back here if he already knew there was someone else in his——?

Release came to her pain-locked body on a shuddering jolt of realisation that had her dropping like a dead weight on to the bed behind her, mouth dry, pulses gone absolutely haywire.

He was angry with her because she hadn't contacted him on the very day their six months was up. He'd been stiff and withdrawn when she'd eventually arrived here, waiting for her to make the next move—next move to what?

To show him why she had come back, she answered her own question. He'd been hurt because she had shown no eagerness to be back, and the hurt had turned into a cold-eyed self-defence.

Hurt, not dented pride. Fear, not anger. Love, not just good old-fashioned lust when his gaze had raked so intensely over her.

Her eyes began to shine—not with tears but with a bright blue elation. Then she laughed, placing both hands on top of her head, and fell backwards across the bed on another shout of ecstatic laughter.

'He loves me!' she whispered tearfully to the ceiling above her. 'Dane Norfolk loves me!'

Feeling dizzy on the power of discovery, she forced herself up off the bed and went for her shower, eager now to get to him, see with her own eyes if it was as real as she was allowing herself to believe it to be.

But what if she was wrong? The smile died suddenly, the feelings of elation with it. What if she was just plucking fantasy out of the air to salve her hungry heart?

No, she refused to so much as tiptoe down that line of thinking, she decided firmly as she came back from the bathroom swathed in one white fluffy towel around her body and another one around her freshly washed hair. She wasn't stupid. She might be madly—incurably in love with the man, but that didn't mean her brain had lost its ability to function.

Dane, cruel and cutting as he could be, was not quite that cruel, she decided as she sat down on the bed and swung the towel from her head to begin towel-drying her hair. He would not have brought her all the way back here just to tell her he was in love with someone else.

'Hmmm.' She stopped rubbing her hair so that she could savour the new wonderful feeling, fizzing with it—actually light-headed with it.

With a habit she had grown into during her six-month separation from him, she hooked up a pillow and curled up on the bed, hugging the pillow to her as she'd always done when thinking of Dane, and let her mind and her senses absorb the new feelings.

She wished she had a giant daisy to hand, she thought fancifully, so she could go the whole romantic hog and pull petals—'He loves me, he loves me not——'

But no, she frowned, deciding that she didn't want to tempt fate with petals which might give her the wrong answer. Instead, she closed her eyes and let the full force of his image encompass her. His hair, black, straight, sleek—itching to be muzzed by her sensual fingers. His face, hard as granite but so attractive that it stopped her heart just to look at it. His eyes, not silver, because she wanted to think of them warm, not cold. So she coloured them grey—like smoke, dark and disturbing as she had seen them when his naked body had lain moulded sensually with hers. And his mouth, warm and passionate, drawing from her the kind of wanton response she had been aching to experience again for six long, miserable months.

Mmm, delicious, beautiful. What dreams were made of...

It was over an hour later that Dane strode impatiently into her room then stopped dead, the deep, burning feelings of anger he had come in here to blast her with fading into a gut-wrenching ache when he saw her curled up on the bed, fast asleep, a pillow clutched lovingly to her breast.

She'd flaked out. While he'd been pacing his lounge, turning himself inside out on a seething mix of anger and need, Lily had calmly showered and then flaked out!

Slowly he approached the bed, then stood looking down at her for a long time, the soft whisper of her steady breathing the only sound in the peaceful room. The towel she had been using on her hair lay crumpled beneath one of her bare feet and he bent down to gently remove it, then found his fingers lingering on the satin smoothness of her skin. She felt cool to the touch, cool enough to catch a chill if he left her sleeping like this.

Unable to resist the temptation, he moved his fingers upwards along her leg, revelling in the sensation of her silk-smooth skin against his fingertips until he came into contact with the damp towel still covering her body. Then gently, so as not to wake her, he unfolded the towel, pulled it free and eased the quilt out from beneath her body, then tried to take the pillow away, only to feel her arms tense around it firmly.

'Dane,' she whispered in her sleep, and a wave of something close to anguish swept over him.

He flicked the duvet over her, then lightly stroked her tousled hair from her brow. It was still touch-damp, smelling cleanly of shampoo. Leaning down, he placed a kiss on her lips, felt them quiver in response, and straightened away ruefully.

Was that quiver because she'd recognised his kiss? Or simply an instinctive response to the feather-light brush of her flesh? He was almost positive it was recognition of him. He was almost positive that she had gone away six months ago heart and soul in love with him.

What he didn't understand was why she had been so reluctant to come back.

Lily came awake with a start, her eyes wide and questioning as they darted around the darkness of her unfamiliar surroundings.

Then she remembered, and relaxed a little. Home; she was home in England. Home with Dane.

The hour was late, she recognised that instinctively, though just how late she had no idea, only that there was something about the silence surrounding her that put the time somewhere in the early hours of the morning.

Someone had put her to bed. She was still clutching her pillow, but she was naked beneath the cosy duvet.

Dane. A smile crept across her sleepy mouth. Dane would have come in and put her to bed. Warmth permeated her belly, a soft, curling kind of warmth that was entirely due to the idea of him gazing on her naked and asleep.

The body of a siren, he used to call it—did he still think she looked like that? She hadn't changed much over the last six months—except for a golden tan she had acquired to her normally pale skin, and that could only improve it, surely?

A sound very like a sigh brought her head swinging sideways on the pillows, and she stopped breathing for a moment, surprised to find she wasn't alone as she'd believed.

Dane was stretched out in a comfy chair beside the bed, his dark head resting against the cushioned back. He had changed out of his business clothes into a dark blue bathrobe and a pair of silk pyjama-bottoms. His eyes were closed and he looked very relaxed, his bare feet resting on the bed just beside her curled-up frame. Languidly she reached out to touch him, her hand curving around his thigh, warm and tautly muscled beneath the fine silk.

He started, then his eyes flicked open, honing directly on to hers.

'Hello,' she greeted shyly.

He didn't say anything for a long moment, perhaps, like her, taking his time to recall where he was. Then, 'Hi,' he answered, and the gruffly sensual sound so lacking in the earlier coldness quivered warmly through her, so she smiled.

'How long have I been asleep?'

Dane glanced at his watch. 'About five hours, give or take.' His tone was indifferent. 'Feeling more—rested now?'

'Mmm,' she murmured, but she was frowning. 'If I've been asleep for that long, that puts the time way past midnight. Why haven't you gone to bed yourself?'

Neither of them had moved since his eyes opened on her. Her hand still rested on his thigh, and his feet were still stretched out on the bed.

'I didn't want to,' he answered casually, and closed his eyes again. 'In fact, I'm quite comfortable where I am. Go back to sleep, Lily, you still look tired.'

'While you sit there?'

He nodded. 'As I said, I'm comfortable here.'

'But it's cold!' she exclaimed. 'And you'll get stiff slouching there like that!'

'I don't slouch,' he denied. 'And I am not cold. So go back to sleep and forget I'm even here.'

Forget he's there? He must be joking! 'But why?' she murmured in bewilderment. 'Why do you want to sit there?'

His shrug was oddly diffident. 'I don't want you trying to sneak away in the early hours of the morning before we've had a chance to—talk.'

'I wouldn't do that,' she protested.

His eyes flicked open, hard and glittering. 'You tried it the last time we were together.'

'That was different.' Lily shifted restlessly.

'Was it? I don't think so.' He shut his eyes again. 'As I said, I'll stay here where I can keep a check on you, if you don't mind.'

Lily chewed gently on her bottom lip, her eyes studying him through the night gloom. He looked tired, and no matter what he claimed he had to be feeling the cold. And there was a grim pallor to his face that hinted that he wasn't as relaxed as he would like her to believe.

A wave of aching love swelled up inside her, warming her eyes and sending her resting hand sliding lightly along his thigh. Beneath her fingers, the muscle tightened on a ripple of reflex response and his eyes flicked open again, dark and guarded suddenly.

'What the hell do you think you're doing?' he gritted.

'Inviting you,' she answered softly.

'Inviting me to what?' he snapped.

Calmly, amazed at her own boldness, Lily shifted her hand to the duvet, lifting it away from her body. 'If you feel you have to hold a watching brief over me, Dane,' she murmured, 'then it would be far more—comfortable if you did it in here—with me.'

His eyes slid down the full curving length of her body, more than half hidden from him by the pillow she was clutching so possessively. He swallowed, and flicked his gaze back to hers.

'What's the pillow for?' he asked. 'Protection from my amorous advances?'

Lily shook her head, her eyes soft. 'The pillow is you,' she told him simply. 'You've hugged me to sleep every night for the last six months.' Deliberately she removed the pillow, letting it slip carelessly to the floor, revealing herself, her skin wearing the lingering blush of sleep. 'I don't think I need it any more.'

'God,' he choked and jerked to his feet. 'God, Lily, you don't know what you're inviting there——' Tension touched his mouth, a hand going up to grip the back of his neck. 'If I get in that bed with you, it won't be to hug you to sleep!'

'I'm so glad,' she drawled. 'I was beginning to wonder if you'd lost your instincts altogether!'

'You want me?' he demanded, ignoring her stab at a joke. 'Even though I treated you so badly when you arrived?'

'I want you,' she confirmed, the duvet still held up invitingly.

'Yet you wouldn't even be here if I hadn't begged you to come back!'

'Take your clothes off and come and get in here with me,' she murmured. 'I'm getting cold lying here like this.'

'For God's sake, Lily! I want to know why you didn't get in touch with me!' he exploded angrily.

'I love you,' she said, and watched him stiffen up like a board before going on quietly. 'I was frightened you might not want me any more. It was easier not coming to find out than taking the pain it would cost me to get here only to find you'd even forgotten my name.'

'Lily,' he murmured shakily, 'I've *always* wanted you! How could you ever have worried otherwise?'

'But you had me, Dane,' she reminded him bluntly. 'And let's face it,' she sighed, letting the duvet drop back over her body, 'I didn't really give you much option.' Her smile was self-derisive on the memory of how utterly she'd thrown herself at him that night. 'I seduced you, not the other way around. You were ready to walk out of that hotel room without so much as touching me if you could avoid it. Oh, you tried to justify it by quoting excuses like my needing time and bad appearances, but really the real cold truth about it was that you *could* walk away. It was me who couldn't let you.'

'I did need time,' he insisted. 'Dammit, Lily, we *both* needed time. What do you think it did to me for those two years, lusting after my own brother's wife?'

'Lust just about says it,' she grimaced, her eyes bleak when she recalled the way they'd made love that night.

'Does it?' His black brows rose grimly. 'I never did tell you the real reason why I came chasing around to your hotel that night, did I?' It was his turn to grimace, his turn to look suddenly bleak. 'Three weeks I'd managed to stay away from the stud. Three bloody awful weeks while I persisted in telling myself that you were no good, weren't worth the sleep I lost over you.' He sighed heavily. 'Then, when I came to the point when I couldn't stay away any longer, I rang you. I wanted to see you—but not there—not at the stud where Daniel's presence was stamped all over the damned place—— ' He sucked in a deep breath and let it out again. 'I was going to ask you to come up to London—to my apartment—to seduce you, Lily, let there be no doubt about that. I was going to slake myself in you until I could slake myself no more! I was going to rid myself of my obsession with my brother's wife and set myself free of it if it killed me. It almost did kill me when Mrs Jakes informed me that you weren't there, that you'd left to go to Australia to visit your parents. God knows what I'd have done, if she hadn't then told me you were spending a night in the airport hotel before catching your plane the next morning.'

'So you came there, spitting out yet more insinuations about me and Mark,' Lily said. 'Not very seductive of you.'

'I was too bloody jealous of Mark Radley to be seductive,' he grunted. 'Having kept tabs on his movements because I wanted to make sure he stayed well away from you, I knew where he'd gone. It was quite a simple step to assume you were going to see him in Hong Kong on your way to your parents. It's the route I always take myself when I go to Australia, you see. So it never occurred to me that you would be going any other way.'

'And you were too busy seeing bad in me to wonder,' she added drily.

'Yes.' Sighing, he came to sit down beside her. His eyes were dark and disturbingly gentle, more gentle than she'd ever seen them. 'Forgive me?' he murmured.

'What is there to forgive?' Unable to resist the need to touch him, she reached up to stroke her fingers through his hair. 'There were so many lies, Dane,' she sighed. 'So many secrets causing so much bitterness and suspicion.'

'I tried to do the honourable thing, you know, and let you go away without touching you.'

'Until I begged.'

Leaning down, he kissed her gently on the lips. 'You only begged for what I was desperate for myself,' he told her. 'It was a joint loss of control. And I revelled in every second of it. It was the most mind-blowing experience of my life. Afterwards— well, everything went a little crazy afterwards.' Grim-faced again, he stood up. 'You didn't spare me at all that night, Lily. And left me feeling punch-drunk for days afterwards, with what you'd told me.'

'I'm sorry if it hurt you, but the lies couldn't go on, Dane. Not after...' She didn't say it, swallowing thickly instead. 'I thought you hated me after that,' she confessed, remembering that cold farewell at the airport, remembering the way he couldn't even bring himself to look at her.

'I could have convinced you to stay,' he said as if reading her own thoughts. 'I could have weathered the storm of speculation that would—and still could—flare up around the kind of relationship we were heading for. But I didn't think you could weather it. You'd taken enough,' he added heavily, 'more than enough of living a lie. I couldn't keep you here and let you take the brunt of everyone's disgust at us. And I couldn't ask you to live another lie by keeping what we were to each other a secret. It was better to let you go. Easier, actually,' he admitted. 'Because at least with half the world between us I wouldn't be tempted to change my mind. But it hit me hard when you made no attempt to contact me as soon as the deadline was up,' he confessed. 'It was something I just hadn't allowed myself to consider—that you would find you could do without me!'

'You were that sure of me?' Tears filled her eyes at how horribly transparent she had been.

'Lily,' Dane sighed, 'you are the most loyal and decent person I have ever known. You would not have given yourself to me if you hadn't cared deeply enough to put all your principles aside—of course I was that sure of you.'

'And y-you still w-want me?'

'Want you?' His sigh this time was raw with pain. 'I've been slowly dying with wanting you over these last rotten six months.'

'Then come to bed,' she invited thickly. 'I need you to show me how much.' With a trembling hand this time, she lifted the duvet again, her huge, tear-filled eyes begging him to come to her.

Dane needed no more persuasion. His eyes began to glow as they held hers, his hands lifting to the knot holding his robe in place. It came away from his body to reveal slick bronzed skin and a rock-solid chest darkly matted with hair. His gaze never leaving hers, he dropped the robe on to the chair, then took the few steps which brought his silk-covered thighs against the bed.

Mouth dry, the air literally pulsing with sexual tension, she looked into the simmering burn of his eyes, and reached out with a hand towards his thigh.

'These, too,' she whispered, lightly brushing the pair of blue silk pyjama-bottoms which was all he had left on him.

His chest rose and fell. Then, with fingers that weren't quite steady, he peeled them away. Lily took her time letting her hungry gaze slide over him. And his smile when she flicked her eyes blushingly back to his was rueful.

'So now you know just how much I want you,' he mocked, and slid himself into the bed beside her.

His skin was cold to the touch, but taut and smooth like satin. Sighing softly, she curled herself into him, felt him do the same, and sighed again as they tangled lovingly.

It was a hectic ascent. It could not be otherwise after such a long, long wait. And they hit that static-filled vortex of absolute oneness before they'd even had chance to savour any of it.

Coming back down to earth was slow and pleasurably sensual, though—a series of lazy, drugging kisses and light, loving caresses.

'I am insanely in love with you, you know,' Dane huskily confessed as he held her locked beneath him.

'I know.' Lily kissed him softly on the lips.

But Dane jerked away. 'You know?' he repeated. 'But how could you know when I haven't so much as hinted at the word love before?' He looked so disappointed at her perception of him that Lily had to hide a smile.

'Dane,' she mocked, 'did you honestly expect me to believe that without love you would still have been here waiting for me after six months? Of course not,' she agreed when he grimaced. 'Which is why the first move had to come from you. You, after all,' she derided, 'had been reading me like an open book from the first moment we met! I had no idea what you really felt for me—whether it was just the evil lust, or a sympathy for the woman your brother had hidden his own problems behind. And—anyway,' she added, tracing his square jaw with a lazy finger, 'Jo-Jo told me.'

'Jo-Jo did what?' he snapped, surprised enough to try to move away from her.

But Lily refused to let him. 'He was only trying to defend your bad temper!' she exclaimed. 'By explaining to me that every man behaves like a boor when he's in love!'

'And you instantly assumed that if I was in love it had to be with you, did you?'

'Glass houses, Dane,' Lily reminded him softly. 'A man with your family sensitivity to a scandal would not set himself up to have stones thrown at him, unless his feelings were deeply involved. Which reminds me.' She frowned suddenly. 'Why did you tell Jo-Jo not to call me Mrs Norfolk any more? Did that have anything to do with the glass houses thing?'

'No.' His smile was suddenly sheepish as he leaned down to kiss her. 'That was to do with me, and my—dislike of having him constantly calling you Mrs Norfolk when you were still the wrong Mrs Norfolk. He can call you it again after we're married,' he promised lightly. 'But not before!'

'So we are going to get married, are we?' It was her turn to sound light, but really Lily's heart had just swelled to bursting.

'Of course,' he frowned. 'I want you tied to me as completely as you were tied to my brother—only much more,' he added huskily. 'Because I'm having all of you—all of you, got that? And to hell with anyone who wants to cast stones at what we are to each other!'

'To hell with the glass houses,' she agreed, and laughed, pulling his mouth firmly on to hers.

MEN · MADE IN AMERICA

**Fifty red-blooded, white-hot, true-blue hunks
from every State in the Union!**

Look for MEN MADE IN AMERICA! Written by some
of our most poplar authors, these stories feature fifty of
the strongest, sexiest men, each from a different state in
the union!

Two titles available every other month at your favorite
retail outlet.

In January, look for:

DREAM COME TRUE by Ann Major (Florida)
WAY OF THE WILLOW by Linda Shaw (Georgia)

In March, look for:

TANGLED LIES by Anne Stuart (Hawaii)
ROGUE'S VALLEY by Kathleen Creighton (Idaho)

You won't be able to resist MEN MADE IN AMERICA!

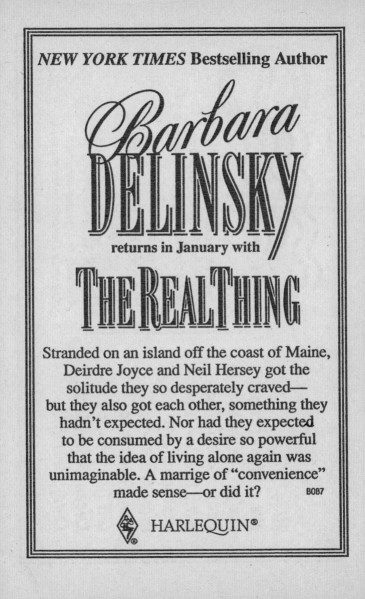

NEW YORK TIMES **Bestselling Author**

Barbara DELINSKY

returns in January with

THE REAL THING

Stranded on an island off the coast of Maine,
Deirdre Joyce and Neil Hersey got the
solitude they so desperately craved—
but they also got each other, something they
hadn't expected. Nor had they expected
to be consumed by a desire so powerful
that the idea of living alone again was
unimaginable. A marrige of "convenience"
made sense—or did it?

BOB7

HARLEQUIN®

Relive the romance...
Harlequin and Silhouette
are proud to present

by Request™

A program of collections of three complete novels by the most requested authors with the most requested themes. Be sure to look for one volume each month with three complete novels by top name authors.

In January:	**WESTERN LOVING**	Susan Fox
		JoAnn Ross
		Barbara Kaye

Loving a cowboy is easy—taming him isn't!

In February:	**LOVER, COME BACK!**	Diana Palmer
		Lisa Jackson
		Patricia Gardner Evans

It was over so long ago—yet now they're calling, "Lover, Come Back!"

In March:	**TEMPERATURE RISING**	JoAnn Ross
		Tess Gerritsen
		Jacqueline Diamond

Falling in love—just what the doctor ordered!

Available at your favorite retail outlet.

REQ-G3

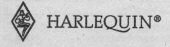

HARLEQUIN® ♥ Silhouette

HARLEQUIN®

Don't miss these Harlequin favorites by some of our most distinguished authors!
And now, you can receive a discount by ordering two or more titles!

HT#25409	THE NIGHT IN SHINING ARMOR by JoAnn Ross	$2.99	☐
HT#25471	LOVESTORM by JoAnn Ross	$2.99	☐
HP#11463	THE WEDDING by Emma Darcy	$2.89	☐
HP#11592	THE LAST GRAND PASSION by Emma Darcy	$2.99	☐
HR#03188	DOUBLY DELICIOUS by Emma Goldrick	$2.89	☐
HR#03248	SAFE IN MY HEART by Leigh Michaels	$2.89	☐
HS#70464	CHILDREN OF THE HEART by Sally Garrett	$3.25	☐
HS#70524	STRING OF MIRACLES by Sally Garrett	$3.39	☐
HS#70500	THE SILENCE OF MIDNIGHT by Karen Young	$3.39	☐
HI#22178	SCHOOL FOR SPIES by Vickie York	$2.79	☐
HI#22212	DANGEROUS VINTAGE by Laura Pender	$2.89	☐
HI#22219	TORCH JOB by Patricia Rosemoor	$2.89	☐
HAR#16459	MACKENZIE'S BABY by Anne McAllister	$3.39	☐
HAR#16466	A COWBOY FOR CHRISTMAS by Anne McAllister	$3.39	☐
HAR#16462	THE PIRATE AND HIS LADY by Margaret St. George	$3.39	☐
HAR#16477	THE LAST REAL MAN by Rebecca Flanders	$3.39	☐
HH#28704	A CORNER OF HEAVEN by Theresa Michaels	$3.99	☐
HH#28707	LIGHT ON THE MOUNTAIN by Maura Seger	$3.99	☐

Harlequin Promotional Titles

#83247	YESTERDAY COMES TOMORROW by Rebecca Flanders	$4.99	☐
#83257	MY VALENTINE 1993	$4.99	☐
	(short-story collection featuring Anne Stuart, Judith Arnold, Anne McAllister, Linda Randall Wisdom)		

(limited quantities available on certain titles)

	AMOUNT	$	
DEDUCT:	10% DISCOUNT FOR 2+ BOOKS	$	
ADD:	POSTAGE & HANDLING	$	
	($1.00 for one book, 50¢ for each additional)		
	APPLICABLE TAXES*	$	_____
	TOTAL PAYABLE	$	_____
	(check or money order—please do not send cash)		

To order, complete this form and send it, along with a check or money order for the total above, payable to Harlequin Books, to: **In the U.S.:** 3010 Walden Avenue, P.O. Box 9047, Buffalo, NY 14269-9047; **In Canada:** P.O. Box 613, Fort Erie, Ontario, L2A 5X3.

Name: _____

Address: _____ City: _____

State/Prov.: _____ Zip/Postal Code: _____

*New York residents remit applicable sales taxes.
Canadian residents remit applicable GST and provincial taxes.

HBACK-JM

My Valentine

1994

Celebrate the most romantic day of the year with
MY VALENTINE 1994
a collection of original stories, written by
four of Harlequin's most popular authors...

MARGOT DALTON
MURIEL JENSEN
MARISA CARROLL
KAREN YOUNG

*Available in February, wherever
Harlequin Books are sold.*

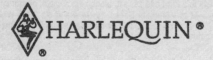

HARLEQUIN ®

VAL94

Share the adventure—and the romance—of

HARLEQUIN ⬥ PRESENTS®

A Year
DOWN UNDER

If you missed any titles in this miniseries,
here's your chance to order them:

Harlequin Presents®—A Year Down Under

#11519	HEART OF THE OUTBACK by Emma Darcy	$2.89	☐
#11527	NO GENTLE SEDUCTION by Helen Blanchin	$2.89	☐
#11537	THE GOLDEN MASK by Robyn Donald	$2.89	☐
#11546	A DANGEROUS LOVER by Lindsay Armstrong	$2.89	☐
#11554	SECRET ADMIRER by Susan Napier	$2.89	☐
#11562	OUTBACK MAN by Miranda Lee	$2.99	☐
#11570	NO RISKS, NO PRIZES by Emma Darcy	$2.99	☐
#11577	THE STONE PRINCESS by Robyn Donald	$2.99	☐
#11586	AND THEN CAME MORNING by Daphne Clair	$2.99	☐
#11595	WINTER OF DREAMS by Susan Napier	$2.99	☐
#11601	RELUCTANT CAPTIVE by Helen Blanchin	$2.99	☐
#11611	SUCH DARK MAGIC by Robyn Donald	$2.99	☐

(limited quantities available on certain titles)

TOTAL AMOUNT	$
POSTAGE & HANDLING	$
($1.00 for one book, 50¢ for each additional)	
APPLICABLE TAXES*	$ _____
TOTAL PAYABLE	$ _____
(check or money order—please do not send cash)	

To order, complete this form and send it, along with a check or money order for the total above, payable to Harlequin Books, to: *In the U.S.*: 3010 Walden Avenue, P.O. Box 9047, Buffalo, NY 14269-9047; *In Canada*: P.O. Box 613, Fort Erie, Ontario, L2A 5X3.

Name: _____

Address: _____City: _____

State/Prov.: _____Zip/Postal Code: _____

*New York residents remit applicable sales taxes.
Canadian residents remit applicable GST and provincial taxes.

YDUF